IN THE LAND OF LEADALE

8

Ceez

[ILLUSTRATION BY]

Tenmaso

YEN ON

NEW YORK

L ✦ IN THE LAND OF ✦ EADALE 8 Ceez

Translation by Jessica Lange
Cover art by Tenmaso

RIADEIRU NO DAICHI NITE Vol. 8
© Ceez 2022
First published in Japan in 2022 by KADOKAWA CORPORATION, Tokyo.
English translation rights arranged with KADOKAWA CORPORATION, Tokyo, through TUTTLE-MORI AGENCY, INC., Tokyo.

English translation © 2023 by Yen Press, LLC

Yen On
150 West 30th Street, 19th Floor
New York, NY 10001

Visit us at yenpress.com
facebook.com/yenpress
twitter.com/yenpress
yenpress.tumblr.com
instagram.com/yenpress

First Yen On Edition: April 2023
Edited by Yen On Editorial: Rachel Mimms
Designed by Yen Press Design: Liz Parlett

Yen On is an imprint of Yen Press, LLC.
The Yen On name and logo are trademarks of Yen Press, LLC.

Library of Congress Cataloging-in-Publication Data
Names: Ceez, author. | Tenmaso, illustrator. | Lange, Jessica (Translator), translator.
Title: In the land of Leadale / Ceez ; illustration by Tenmaso ; translation by Jessica Lange
Other titles: Riadeiru no daichi nite. English
Description: First Yen On edition. | New York, NY : Yen On, 2020.
Identifiers: LCCN 2020032160 | ISBN 9781975308681 (v. 1 ; trade paperback) |
    ISBN 9781975308704 (v. 2 ; trade paperback) | ISBN 9781975322168 (v. 3 ; trade paperback) |
    ISBN 9781975322182 (v. 4 ; trade paperback) | ISBN 9781975333447 (v. 5 ; trade paperback) |
    ISBN 9781975334598 (v. 6 ; trade paperback) | ISBN 9781975343910 (v. 7 ; trade paperback) |
    ISBN 9781975360993 (v. 8 ; trade paperback)
Subjects: CYAC: Fantasy. | Virtual reality—Fiction.
Classification: LCC PZ7.1.C4646 In 2020 | DDC [Fic]—dc23
LC record available at https://lccn.loc.gov/2020032160

ISBNs: 978-1-9753-6099-3 (paperback)
        978-1-9753-6100-6 (ebook)

10 9 8 7 6 5 4 3 2 1

LSC-C

Printed in the United States of America

IN THE LAND OF LEADALE

8

IN THE LAND OF LEADALE CONTENTS

ILLUSTRATION BY Tenmaso

Cayna

Also known as the Silver Ring Witch, she was a top player of the VRMMORPG *Leadale* back in its heyday. Became an adventurer upon getting reincarnated two hundred years after the game's service ended.

Skargo

Eldest of the three NPC children Cayna raised in the Game Era. Now the High Priest, this peerless beauty is outranked only by the king and prime minister. Constantly uses Oscar—Roses Scatter with Beauty to adorn himself with flowers, ocean waves, and sound effects.

Mai-Mai

Skargo's younger elven sister who specializes in attack magic. In this world, she is a former Imperial Mage who currently serves as headmaster of the Royal Academy. Constantly bickering with Skargo, although they both love Cayna above all else.

Kartatz

A dwarf and the youngest of Cayna's three adopted children. A master builder whose fortresses, castles, and dungeons are second to none, he has more common sense than Skargo and Mai-Mai combined.

Marelle

The proprietress of the inn where Cayna first awoke. Acts like a second mother to her.

Lytt

Marelle's daughter who helps run the family inn. Looks up to Cayna like a big sister.

Elineh

An astute kobold merchant and caravan leader. Disconcerted by Cayna's terrible business sense, he drills the basics into her while relying on her skills as an adventurer.

Luka

The sole survivor of her fishing village after it was razed by a ghost ship. Cayna decided to adopt her, and now they live together in the remote village.

Roxilius

Cayna's diligent butler. He teaches Luka and the other village children reading, writing, and arithmetic.

Roxine

Cayna's maid who oversees the housework and helps look after Luka. She and Roxilius fight like cats and dogs.

Opus
(Opuskettenshultheimer Crosstettbomber)

Cayna's friend and partner since the game's beta phase. A carefree demon and special kind of idiot. However, in truth, he is also a skilled tactician once known as Leadale's Kongming.

Siren

Opus's maid summons who has the courage to serve a troublemaker like Opus.

The Story Thus Far

After a terrible accident left her permanently confined to a hospital bed, Keina Kagami enjoyed the only life still open to her within the VRMMORPG *Leadale*. Unfortunately, however, she died one day after a power surge short-circuited the equipment keeping her alive. A split second later, Keina woke up in an unfamiliar room and realized with shock that she looked just like her high elf avatar, Cayna.

After talking with the young girl Lytt, who had come to wake her and her mother, the inn proprietress Marelle, Keina was dumbfounded to discover this world was similar to *Leadale* except two hundred years in the future. Relieved to still have her AI support, Kee, Keina decided to embrace this new life and live as her avatar Cayna.

First, Cayna reawakened her Guardian Tower and, at the Guardian's request, decided to set out on an international journey to rouse the other dormant towers. However, her basic knowledge of this world was iffy at best. It was Elineh, the kobold leader of a merchant caravan, and Arbiter, the captain of the Flame Spear mercenaries hired to protect them, who showed Cayna the ropes after the three met in the remote village.

In the royal capital of Felskeilo, Cayna registered with the

Adventurers Guild. It wasn't long before an old knight named Agaido and his granddaughter Lonti personally asked her to catch a young boy darting around town who, as it turned out, happened to be Felskeilo's runaway prince. In addition to receiving compensation from Agaido, Cayna also gained the support of the aristocracy.

Cayna next set out to meet her three children: the High Priest Skargo, the Royal Academy headmistress Mai-Mai, and the master shipbuilder Kartatz. She managed to reunite with Kartatz first, but it was no easy feat. Thrilled by their first interaction in this world, Cayna mentioned that she had joined the Adventurers Guild and told him not to be a stranger.

Kartatz later held a telepathic family meeting with Skargo and Mai-Mai to let them know Cayna was in the capital. As Kartatz and Mai-Mai discussed what they could do for their mother, they also kept a concerned eye on their eldest brother Skargo's wild antics.

As Cayna learned her way around the city, she reunited with Mai-Mai while on a Guild request and was stunned to learn her daughter was married. Later on, she visited the Battle Arena as part of a different request and discovered it was the location of another Guardian Tower. Her heart swelled with excitement, but this all came crashing down when the tower's smoky Guardian disclosed the parting words and disappearance of its Skill Master.

As Cayna grappled with the shocking realization that she was the only player left in this world, her eldest, Skargo, fired up his skill effects and rushed to her side. However, one uppercut from his confused mother sent the High Priest headfirst into the ceiling. Cayna erected an impenetrable barrier around herself, so Mai-Mai and Kartatz had no choice but to collect their brother and leave her be.

Afterward, Skargo went wild for a completely different reason that sent Mai-Mai off the deep end. The two began to shoot ferocious spells at each other, and a sibling battle quickly broke out. As Kartatz rushed to escape the violence, he spotted his mother (who had locked herself away) buying street food without a care in the world, and he couldn't help but miserably wonder what the heck the three of them had been so worried about.

Cayna subdued the family feud and apologized for neglecting her children. All three forgave her with smiles, and everyone vowed to come together and be a happy family once more.

Elineh then asked Cayna to escort his caravan as a guard, and they prepared to head for Helshper to the north. Mai-Mai came to see her mother off and asked Cayna to deliver a letter. She willingly accepted, but little did Cayna know of the pandemonium it would stir within her only a few days later.

The caravan stopped by a remote village on the way, and Cayna rescued the mermaid Mimily, who had become lost in the underground waterways. Once the situation was cleared up and everyone was back on the road, they came to a fallen bridge. Luckily, Cayna cast a spell that allowed everyone to walk on water and make it to the other side.

At the fortress along the national border, they were "warmly" welcomed by a group of bandits from the west. However, Cayna and the Flame Spears made short work of them and safely arrived in Helshper.

While in the city, Cayna visited a shop called Sakaiya to deliver Mai-Mai's letter. It was addressed to the company's founder, Caerick, who happened to be Mai-Mai's son and, by extension, Cayna's grandson. After a slight disagreement, Cayna ran out of the shop in a huff and met a female knight who was investigating the incident at the border. Her name was Caerina, and Cayna's inner turmoil reached new heights upon the realization she was twice a grandmother.

Cayna stopped by the Adventurers Guild and then decided to ask

Caerick for his help, despite earlier tensions. Elineh had mentioned the location of a possible Guardian Tower in bandit territory, and she was dying to check it out.

A group of rock golems attacked the knights just as Cayna arrived on the front lines, but she managed to step in and save them from the brink of annihilation. As a show of thanks, Caerina allowed Cayna to enter the fortress. She soon found the Guardian Tower and fought one-on-one with the former demon player turned bandit leader. He believed everything was still a game until Cayna drilled the truth into him. The outmatched demon began to cry and wail as she prepared to deal the finishing blow.

At the very last second, the demon player's life was spared by Caerina and her Helshper knights. Cayna handed him over to avoid confrontation but limited his power with a collar. It was then the demon player realized she was a Skill Master.

Inside the tower, Cayna was dumbfounded when the reawakened Guardian informed her that Opus was its appointed Skill Master. He was a former fellow guild member and pretty terrible friend, but she still hoped he was alive in this world. Opus's air of mystery deepened further when a fairy visible only to Cayna popped out of a book the Guardian entrusted to her.

After helping her son Kartatz fix a bridge on the way back to Felskeilo, Cayna took on a hunting request for the Adventurers Guild. As she prepared to leave, she ran into Lonti and Lonti's friend Mye. The two ended up joining Cayna and were treated to an endless series of incredible feats.

Back in Felskeilo, Lopus was desperate to replicate Cayna's skills and tossed one of his failed experiments into a garbage pit. Unfortunately, this was both a disputed point from the game's Battle Events and the spawn point of a monster known to drop a special item. By a stroke of unbelievable coincidence, it reacted to the contents of the pit and summoned a dolphin-headed penguin monster.

Two players sprang into action as mass chaos befell Felskeilo. Oddly enough, Shining Saber and Cohral were former guildmates who had coincidentally reunited right before the incident. The duo's skills were sadly no match for the monster, however, and they were injured in a counterattack. Even the nation's best mages couldn't leave a scratch.

Thanks to Li'l Fairy's grim intuition, Cayna sensed the danger and dealt with it from beyond the city. Struck by the full brunt of her magic, the monster vanished in a pillar of fire.

After the incident, Cayna heard the inside scoop about the game's demise from Shining Saber and Cohral. The latter also mentioned a Guardian Tower sunken in the waters around Felskeilo, and she transferred a skill to him as a thank-you.

Cayna arrived in the remote village for a quick visit but negotiated with the elder when a sudden invitation inspired her to take up residence. She met a group of researchers from Otaloquess as well. They were accompanied by a pair of sibling adventurers who served as muscle, and the younger sister suffered a mighty defeat after picking a fight with Cayna.

After watching his sister fail, the older brother Cloffe's demeanor instantly shifted. He fell to one knee as an emissary of Otaloquess and informed Cayna that Queen Sahalashade was her niece. She was a Foster Child of Sahana, a former member of the high elf community who was like a little sister to Cayna. Cayna turned down Cloffe's solicitation and shuddered at how everyone she ran into seemed to have deep government ties.

Cayna returned to Felskeilo and decided to join a group of knights who set out to crush the remaining bandits. Thanks to a bit of friendly banter, the knights mistakenly got the idea she and Shining Saber were engaged.

After overcoming an ambush and leaving the knights, Cayna entered a fishing village shrouded in a suspicious fog. As she wandered the unsettling, zombie-infested hamlet, Cayna met another adventurer named Quolkeh, who had come to investigate. She and another familiar face were protecting a young girl, the village's sole survivor, in an underground storehouse. Cayna had previously asked the two for directions in the Adventurers Guild back in Helshper, and both were confirmed players.

Quolkeh's partner was a dragoid and an old friend from Cayna's Cream Cheese guild back in the game. He went by Exis these days but once played a sensible character named Tartarus on his main account. As Cayna and Exis continued to catch up, the trio made every effort to safeguard the girl. Cayna summoned a butler named Roxilius to watch over her, and everyone utilized their abilities as players to make short work of the enemy. The ghost ship and its underlings crumbled away in a matter of moments.

After awakening the Dragon Palace of the Fifth Skill Master, Cayna decided to adopt the young girl who had lost her home and family. She summoned a maid named Roxine to lend a hand and brought Luka to live with her in the remote village.

Not long after their move-in date, Cayna fulfilled a longtime promise to Lytt and summoned a creature to take her and the children on a scenic flight. Along the way, she saved Arbiter and the Flame Spears from a vicious monster attack. With the help of a magical item, Cayna realized that quest enemies were lurking in the area around the village and teamed up with the Flame Spears to eliminate them. However, a simultaneous incident occurred when Luka, Lytt, and Latem sneaked out of the village on their own.

Just as a horde of monsters surrounded the children in the

meadow, a White Dragon came to their rescue. Cayna had given it to Luka as a protective charm, and the beast's breath attack left deep scars in the forest as it scattered the enemy. Cayna rushed back to the village to confirm their safety.

Cayna next headed to Sakaiya to pick up a few daily necessities. While there, she also took the opportunity to introduce her great-grandson, Idzik, to Cohral and his party, who had come to discuss a request from the Adventurers Guild. Caerick informed Cayna that a conference would be held on the national border. Back in the village, Skargo greeted his mother and announced he had come to attend the meeting as the king's representative.

Cayna and Roxilius later worked together to bolster the village's defenses and packed enough firepower to kill even a player in an instant.

To expand Lytt's and Luka's horizons, Cayna decided to bring the girls along with her to Felskeilo. Roxine accompanied them, and everyone rode together in a remodeled golem wagon alongside Elineh's caravan. However, the rarity of Cayna's transport had also drawn the attention of troublesome nobles, and Elineh warned that she was secretly being targeted.

Meanwhile, they arrived in Felskeilo right in the middle of the city's River Festival. Unfortunately, the main festivities were put on hold, thanks to a large mysterious shadow spotted in the Ejidd River, and an air of confusion lingered over the town. Cayna set out to eliminate this dark phantom at the request of the Adventurers Guild.

They rented a house from Elineh's company as a base of operations while in Felskeilo, so Cayna left the children with Roxine and another summons as she set out to investigate the river. Meanwhile, a nobleman hired an underworld organization to kidnap Cayna's loved ones, but Roxine protected the children from harm and thoroughly walloped the punks.

Two fiends sent by an unknown source greeted the men upon their return to the hideout. These surprise visitors inflicted gruesome atrocities upon them and sent each spiraling into despair as they were twisted into grotesque works of art. When these sickly masterpieces were discovered and one revealed the name of the devilish perpetrator, the knights went on high alert.

Cayna finally uncovered the truth of the unsettling shadow, thanks to a summons from the Guardian of the Battle Arena Tower and it wasn't long before her Guardian Ring led her to the mobile Guardian Tower that had swum upstream from the ocean. Cayna devised an outlandish plan to keep the giant white whale in Felskeilo and even used her connections to get the knights and princess involved. When all was said and done, the whale tower became a divine messenger who permanently resided upstream of the sandbar.

Finally free of their woes, Felskeilo's citizens rejoiced as the River Festival kicked into high gear. Cayna enjoyed herself alongside the children but got into a tussle with an arrogant noble when she stopped by the Academy. Nonetheless, he didn't stand a chance against a magical Limit Breaker/Skill Master and earned himself a hearty smackdown.

As the festive air continued into the night, a demon and his hellish lackeys attacked the noble who tried to mess with Cayna. His fate was decided by a single coin toss.

Cayna visited Kartatz's workshop on the sandbar to thank him for the lumber she used to build her home in the remote village. While the children observed the boatbuilding process, Cayna decided to kill time and go fishing. After reeling in multiple huge catches, she finally nabbed a chimera-like monster. Cayna defeated it with ease but realized her prize was some kind of chimera Event Monster after it dropped a rare ore.

Cayna ran into Cohral and Skargo on the road back to the village but found Roxilius groveling in the entranceway upon her return. He held a single letter that simply said, *"Name it."*

Realizing this command meant Li'l Fairy, Cayna named her Kuu, since she seemed like Kee's little sister. While introducing Kuu to the villagers, Cayna was baffled to learn that fairies supposedly brought good luck. When Caerick called upon her over a matter of wholesale magical tools, she introduced Kuu to both him and Idzik and accepted his request in exchange for convenience.

At the same time, she received an urgent player-only message from Shining Saber that said monsters were attacking Felskeilo. She dashed over to Felskeilo's east gate and quickly saved a group of soldiers who struggled to fend off ptera from the Dinosaur Series. Once Cayna pummeled these, she told everyone to take shelter and then set out to crush the main enemy forces. After going all out to curtail the monster horde, Cayna sent the crimson pig Li'l P ahead to defend the west gate against the approaching detached column.

Meanwhile, one of Otaloquess's biggest tourist attractions, a giant tortoise, had gone wild and was headed straight for the royal castle. Knights and adventurers alike were recruited to combat this dire threat, and they decided to contact whoever lived on top of the tortoise's shell and ask them to alter its path. Quolkeh and Exis were involved as well, thanks to a request from the Adventurers Guild. They were coincidentally joined by an old dwarf named Hidden Ogre, who also happened to be a Skill Master, and the trio entered the building atop the tortoise's back. Inside was a TV studio. A delinquent Buddha Guardian recognized them as game show contestants and initiated a slow, agonizing trial. Quolkeh lost halfway through, but Exis and Hidden Ogre managed to answer correctly within the time limit. The giant tortoise stopped within a hair's breadth of Otaloquess's castle.

Elsewhere, Felskeilo was still under attack, and an incident broke out when a peculiar monster took control of the knights and pitted them against the adventurers. However, the adventurers had long tired of the knights' daily arrogance, and with a little instigation from Arbiter (who had also joined the fray), they incapacitated the knights by venting their pent-up grievances. Cayna soon made her entrance with Li'l P and exterminated the monster mastermind.

Cayna set up a meeting with Skargo (who had retreated to the rearguard in the previous battle) but was taken aback when the royal family decided to join them. The king and queen thanked her for watching over the prince and princess and defending the capital. Hoping to learn more about Opus's whereabouts, Cayna questioned Skargo about the Night Sanctuary from Kuu's memories. Unfortunately, it was all for naught.

However, after reviewing her own memories and realizing she'd misheard the name, Cayna quickly determined his location. She and Opus had built a dungeon as a way to mess with new players, and Cayna was surprised to find a village for would-be challengers had built up around it in present-day Otaloquess

In Otaloquess, Cayna ran into the werecat siblings Cloffe and Clofia, whom she'd first met back in the remote village. They decided to tag along for some reason, and the four (Kuu included) descended into the dungeon. Along the way, Clofia's attitude did a sudden one-eighty when her brother mentioned that Cayna was the aunt of her beloved queen. Clofia's subsequent guilt led her straight into a trap.

Cayna blasted through each dungeon floor to save her and finally arrived at bottommost level. However, a midboss demon stood in her way. In the heat of battle, his careless words triggered Cayna's trauma and sent her into a blind fury. She vanquished the demon with a simultaneous rush of Special Skills.

Then, she at last reunited with Opus in the deepest depths of the dungeon. However, his anticlimactic response sent her into yet another frenzy.

Joined by Kuu, Cayna swooped down on Opus with her most powerful spells but collapsed after the earlier Special Skills sapped her MP. Opus ironically saved her and led the group to a hidden house in a corner of the dungeon village. He then left Cayna in the care of his elf maid, Siren, and disappeared. He had secretly gone to meet the owner of a tool shop in the dungeon village who also happened to be a former player. The two vowed to cooperate someday and soon parted.

Cayna took a leisurely wagon trip back to the remote village, but Opus hit her with a number of gut-wrenching revelations along the way.

For instance, he said that the VRMMO *Leadale* was created specifically for Keina. Not only that, he added that Cayna came to this world right after her physical death and had been sleeping in that dungeon for two hundred years prior to being tossed into the village inn. The game system had also synchronized with Cayna's soul while she was napping, and Kuu actually controlled the subsystem. Incidentally, Cayna noticed how suspiciously friendly Kee and Opus acted around each other, but the two brushed off all questions.

Meanwhile, Caerina visited the former player/bandit leader, who now labored in the mines, and invited him to become a soldier.

After returning to the remote village, Cayna introduced Opus and Siren to Roxilius, Roxine, and Luka. Siren harshly disciplined the Double Rs for their constant bickering, accused both of neglecting their duties, and soon became head maid of Cayna's household. The village held a welcome banquet for Opus, where he and Cayna served as the night's entertainment.

The next day, Opus explained to Cayna how the game world became connected to this present one. She later flew with Luka to Opus's tower. Because of this, there was no doubt the game system allowed Cayna to form a party with Luka and any other average person.

Once Cayna and her group arrived in Helshper, Siren informed them via telepathy that Helshper knights had come to the village.

Cayna later reunited with Elineh and Arbiter at the inn and introduced them to Opus before heading off to the castle. Opus instead brought Kuu and Luka with him to the Adventurers Guild, and the three ran into Quolkeh and Exis. Opus wasted no time teasing the dragoid, just like in the good old days.

When Cayna reached the castle, Caerina led her to the knights and said she had invited the former bandit leader/player to join their number. She asked Cayna to remove his Punishment Collar so he could operate at full capacity.

After Cayna removed the collar of the demon player/ex-bandit leader Luvrogue and mercilessly toyed with him as payback, she left Helshper alongside Elineh's caravan. After hearing about a tourney, she asked Opus about remotely broadcasting the event with a magic item. Sadly, Cayna couldn't believe her ears when she heard that their guild base, which had stored a plethora of useful items, had been destroyed on the game's final day.

For a brief moment, Cayna and Opus enjoyed life in the peaceful remote village with their respective servants. Then, one day, Cayna made up her mind to upgrade an item known as a Pair of Eyes, which could display images from one Eye to another. This would allow multiple villagers to enjoy distant sight and sound. She checked each tower's Item Box for a projector, a special accessory item that could display visuals from a Pair of Eyes on a large screen and also play sound.

While switching from one tower to the next, Cayna noticed something odd about the mobile tortoise tower. It was a mere step away from Otaloquess Castle. Just as she was about to try to move it, Sahalashade, the Foster Child of the player Cayna had considered a little sister, jumped from the castle. The two reunited for the first time in two hundred years, and Opus and Cayna worked together to transport the tortoise successfully to the dungeon village.

Both the issue of the tortoise and the Pair of Eyes were finally resolved, and Cayna later heard from Skargo that the tourney would soon begin. Her troubles only grew when her fears came true and Opus decided to enter.

Cayna next took on a request for the Adventurers Guild, and the tourney launched safely (?) after she prevented a few disgraceful players from slipping in.

Even so, when players Shining Saber and Cohral went head-to-head with the ultimate swords they'd received from Cayna, the aftermath destroyed the Battle Arena and subsequently ruined the tourney.

Then, a young man who had been harboring a deep grudge against Opus since the Game Era appeared with a group of summoned beasts. He commanded them to attack the demon, but none listened to a word he said, since Cayna was their original creator. His revenge against Opus failed miserably.

A temporary festival replaced the tourney, and peace returned to the capital...

Prologue

"*Sigh*. Never would've guessed *you* were the one secretly behind this last incident."

"Any Skill Master could have done the same, right? I simply beat everyone to the punch."

A lone island floated in the sky, and on it presided an old single-story samurai house. Hedges surrounded the residence, and there was a small vegetable garden in the courtyard. Several flowerpots sat under the eaves, morning glories bloomed in profusion, and bright crimson berries dangled from Chinese lantern plants. An eye-catching cherry blossom tree flourished by the front entrance, while out back there stood an impressive persimmon tree full of ripe fruit. An abundance of summer vegetables like cucumbers and tomatoes grew in the garden. It was anyone's guess as to what the current season was.

Opus was sharing a drink with an old dwarf on the mansion's veranda. This dwarf was merely old at heart, however; in dwarf years, he was a real whippersnapper. All the same, he had a stocky build and a shaggy beard, and his stern features made it difficult to discern his true age.

This was Hidden Ogre, the Twelfth Skill Master who oversaw the Guardian Tower on this floating island garden.

The isle was compact and didn't extend much farther than the cozy mansion and small yard. The hedges sat on a perimeter that dropped off like a steep cliff.

A white cat with a red collar was sprawled out on the sunlit veranda where the men sat. It stretched lazily and let out a big yawn.

This cat was the Guardian of the aerial garden tower. This tiny, lovable creature happened to speak human languages and was completely invincible within its domain. Anyone careless enough to steal from the vegetable garden would be jettisoned off the island with a single swipe of the feline's paw.

Two women joined Opus and Hidden Ogre. The first was a demon who was watering the garden. Peeking from her reddish brown hair was a pair of small horns characteristic of demonkind. Clad in long brown robes, she paused every once in a while to glance over at Opus and Hidden Ogre. She looked away whenever their eyes almost met, although Opus didn't really mind.

The second woman was a kimono-clad elf who flitted between the house and the veranda with appetizers to pair with the men's *sake*. Pale silver hair complemented her light blue kimono; her demeanor was like a cool, refreshing spring.

"Please enjoy these at your leisure, Sir Opus," she said, setting down the tray of food and bowing elegantly.

"Thanks," said Opus. "Will do."

The elf demonstrated impeccable hospitality without a shred of ill will toward Opus. He smiled in satisfaction, and Hidden Ogre shot him a boastful look.

"So, what do you think of my little sister?" Hidden Ogre asked. "Radiant, ain't she? Bet you're already captivated, ain'tcha?"

"Oh my. You are too much, Big Brother." The elf woman's voice tinkled like a bell. She hid a smile behind her kimono sleeve.

She was indeed Hidden Ogre's younger sister. Or at least one of the Foster Children he'd created. The demon woman tending the garden was another little sister/Foster Child. Her feverish nods alongside Hidden Ogre seemed to demonstrate sisterly pride.

Opus, meanwhile, appeared disenchanted. He silently narrowed his eyes before eventually muttering, "...The world may have changed, but you're as constant as they come."

Hidden Ogre broke into a huge grin and gave a thumbs-up. "What better way to stay young than to be surrounded by pretty girls, right?"

"That wasn't a compliment..."

Hidden Ogre was the only Skill Master who could exasperate Opus like this. Just then, a concerned frown came over the relaxed dwarf's face.

"Do we gotta?" Hidden Ogre asked as he took another sip.

"If nothing is done, a destructive legacy will bite through that barrier and come crawling out."

Although usually passive, Opus wore a grave expression. All jokes aside, this wasn't a situation they could simply ignore.

"We've got a rough idea of how many players are left. The question now is how many will join the fight," Hidden Ogre replied.

"Hmph. There's no coming back if you die in this world, so most hold their lives dear."

"If worse comes to worst, I guess the three of us will just have to use whatever we can summon."

"That might be more terrifying than anything else..."

Hidden Ogre called to his one sister who had turned to leave, since their discussion was clearly an important one.

"Lu Peixi."

The elf woman turned around. "Yes, Big Brother?"

"How long d'you think it'll take to rally everyone?"

"'Everyone'? Forgive my forwardness, but do you intend to start a war somewhere?"

"Not exactly… You might say we're gatherin' reinforcements. Like a rearguard. It'll really help us out if you can join the front in a pinch."

Hidden Ogre glanced over at Opus, and his eyes pleaded for the demon to back him up. However, Opus only nodded as if to say *Do as you please.*

The two were good friends alike in both skill level and mindset, and they could communicate easily without exchanging a single word. Granted, there were a few slight differences between them.

Hidden Ogre didn't yet have a clear picture of the situation and was hesitant to involve his sisters in an uncertain battle.

The demon woman who overheard this conversation left the vegetable garden and trotted over to them.

"Are we gonna go to war, Elder Brother?" she asked, eyes shimmering.

"Like I said, everyone will be backup. You sure look excited, Yunio."

Amid Yunio's childlike demeanor was plenty of anticipation.

"It's been ages since I used Attack Magic to make things go *BAM* and *KABOOM!*" she squealed.

"Sounds a bit like Cayna," Opus muttered. This exchange was giving him déjà vu.

Suddenly, Yunio locked her eyes on him, sending a slight chill down Opus's spine. He flinched; that sweet, innocent gaze harbored a borderline insane fervor.

"Lady Cayna's here? Where? Can I see her? I wanna see Lady Cayna! Let me see her!"

Yunio got right up in his face. There was something terrifying about her vacant golden eyes. Opus had his suspicions about this obsession. He fixed Hidden Ogre with a pointed glare.

"…Hey, Hidden Ogre. What's this foster kid's backstory?"

"Ah, my apologies, Sir Opus," Lu Peixi replied. "She's quite fond of Lady Cayna."

"…Huh." He nodded.

Lu Peixi then proceeded to grab Yunio by the nape with a practiced hand and drag her away from Opus.

"Now, Big Brother," she began, "I believe it will take at least ten days for everyone to properly assemble."

"Right. I'll leave you to it, then."

"Very well."

Once Lu Peixi calmed the madly grinning Yunio, they held hands and approached the white cat on the veranda. In only a few short words, the Guardian sent the pair outside.

Hidden Ogre bade them farewell with a satisfied nod, but Opus looked exhausted.

"You put something like *Admires Cayna* for that girl's flavor text, didn't you? There's no way she'd be so obsessed otherwise."

"Sorry 'bout that. There was a minimum character requirement, so I couldn't just leave it blank. It's not as bad as it looks."

"Eh, I suppose it's not my problem."

Had Cayna been there, she definitely would have begged Opus to ask more questions.

Since neither got the sense they'd be in trouble later, Opus and Hidden Ogre decided to sweep the issue under the rug. In any case, their focus was elsewhere entirely.

"So we'll have at least twenty-three people on our side. Better than nothing, right?" Hidden Ogre said.

"I appreciate the help. I suppose that means you've still got twenty little sisters left..."

"I only regret not including more long-lived races."

Hidden Ogre let out a hearty guffaw, and Opus grimaced.

Determining the Root Cause, a Capture, an Interrogation, and a Breakthrough Strategy

In a reserved room of a certain tavern in Felskeilo's capital, two men collapsed on the table in despair.

"Damn, how'd it come to this...?"

"His Majesty was furious, and it only got worse from there..."

"Don't drag me here out of nowhere and start sulking. It's not like you had no idea what would happen!"

Across from Shining Saber and Cohral, a resentful Cayna sat with her arms folded.

Several days had passed since the tourney ended in total disaster. The city decided to throw together a last-minute festival to ease the spectators' disappointment.

Shining Saber and Cohral had just finished cleaning up their mess and dragged Cayna to this tavern. It was one of the capital's most high-end establishments and a popular choice among adventurers looking to celebrate after a big job. Royal and aristocratic patrons visiting incognito, as well as the successful merchants who frequented the restaurant, were evidence of its fame. Elineh would have fit right in but preferred more modest fare.

Similarly, Shining Saber's last visit to this establishment had

entailed a wild celebration of his promotion to knight captain—this was only his second time here. Cohral was a midlevel adventurer but still preferred to go elsewhere for the sake of his purse strings.

"To think *this* is how I'd end up here…," Shining Saber grumbled.

"Quit it! I can see your eyes glazing over!" Cayna chided.

"This couldn't get any worse. The tourney was a grade-A disaster, so rumors are spreading like wildfire," Cohral added.

"I've heard a few whispers, too. Let's see…," Cayna began.

"Stop! Don't you dare say it!" he cried.

"Oh, you mean the Black Silver Knight and the Supreme Swordsman?"

""GWAAAAAAAAGH?!""

These figures at the center of fresh rumors in the capital were the monikers Shining Saber and Cohral had earned after going berserk (?) in the tourney. Those names made the duo grip their heads and writhe in paralyzed agony.

"Now you've gotten a taste of my pain, right?" said Cayna.

"Y-yeah…"

"So much it hurts…"

The Silver Ring Witch moniker had reached far and wide back in the day. It was Cayna's alias of sorts, and it was even added to her stats as a title once her reputation spread among the player community. Shining Saber and Cohral were similarly the talk of the town, although Felskeilo's current population didn't hold a candle to the number of players during the Game Era.

The system within Cayna's soul failed to update the men's profiles with their new monikers. She checked just to be sure, but there was no mistake. That said, it would've worked only if the system counted normal citizens as players. Cayna had no deliberate control over this, so alas, she could do nothing more than stand by and observe these developments.

"Where's the Supreme part come from anyway...?" Cohral muttered as his shoulders slumped.

"Hmm...," Cayna mused with crossed arms. "If I had to guess, it has something to do with your sword."

Cohral wielded the Holy Warrior Soul Valhalla. The blade shone silver, but apparently it had appeared pure white to spectators during the tourney. And thus, the Supreme Swordsman was born. The weapon was already a hot topic in the Adventurers Guild, and rumors claimed it had produced a powerful gale.

Plus, Cayna had given the Sycophant Sword Runberserk to Shining Saber. This blade, an inky black color, contrasted against Shining Saber's silver scales, earning him the moniker the Black Silver Knight. His knights happened to take a liking to it; Shining Saber, on the other hand, did not appreciate the shift from "Captain" to "O Great Black Silver Knight."

"You two sure had a fun little swordfight," said Cayna.

"Y-you've got it all wrong. It was more like everyone was invisible except Cohral."

"S-same for me. I felt like I had to fight Shining Saber no matter what... I guess you could call it a sense of duty?" Cohral fumbled as he recalled the chaos.

"Actually, yeah. That sounds about right, huh?" Shining Saber agreed.

"Umm, I don't get it. You mean your subconscious forced you or something?"

"Not sure," Cohral admitted.

"It's like my naked sword was in my hand, then suddenly I was fightin' Cohral. Everything was nuts, and I had no idea what was going on. Now that I think about it, no real knight would attack without checking his surroundings first."

"Uh-huh."

"I also shouldn't have rushed into the heat of battle without any thought for my comrades," said Cohral. "Later on, everyone said I went crazy as soon as our fight began…"

"You both congratulated each other, though."

"What else were we supposed to say?!" Shining Saber exclaimed.

"It was a desperate attempt to break the tension…"

Cohral and Shining Saber had fallen to pieces once the match finally ended, and Opus had knocked them down a peg.

Unable to simply brush off the incident, Cohral had groveled before his comrades, while Shining Saber had been visibly uncomfortable without his trusted subordinates by his side. Not that his fellow knights could have stayed there with him, as they'd been tasked with evacuating everyone—in no small part because of Shining Saber himself.

"At any rate, I'm not sure how one swordfight could've created such a massive storm," Cayna mused.

"What do you mean?"

"C'mon, Shining Saber. I think you already know this, but I'm the one who caught that bandit leader a little while ago…"

"Oh yeah, I heard a few details. You handed him over to the Helshper knights, right?"

"That guy was a player," Cayna revealed.

"What?!" Cohral cried in abject shock.

Shining Saber face-palmed. "Seriously…?"

"Let's ignore the fact he was a player for a second," Cayna went on. "He and I had a pretty intense battle, but even we didn't kick up a whirlwind like that. I doubt that happened just because you're both players."

"The poor guy had to go against *you*?" said Shining Saber. "Tough break."

"He hadn't yet realized that I'm a Limit Breaker," she replied wryly.

"Yeah, no one would know you're a tank just by looking at you," Cohral said with a shrug.

"Think either of your weapons had anything to do with it?" Shining Saber asked.

"I had my magic staff, and he used a Hungry Like the Wolf Sword. The staff is basically the same as a Valhalla, while the sword is a gag weapon, so I doubt that's much help to us."

The trio began brainstorming other possible causes, but it turned out to be a hopeless endeavor. If even someone like Cayna, who knew *Leadale* inside and out, didn't know the answer, their prospects were bleak.

"Magic can create storms, right?" Shining Saber asked.

"There's Weather Manipulation, but it's purely ceremonial," Cayna explained. "Besides, a spell like that isn't accurate enough to target the Battle Arena. If you used it in the capital, we'd have a disaster of epic proportions on our hands."

Ceremonial Magic could be cast by several people over a wide area. Only those who possessed the skill could invoke it, of course, and they had to stay in place when casting it. Furthermore, the effects lasted for over a day. Someone with near-infinite MP like Cayna could likely handle the spell herself, but it wouldn't serve any purpose.

"Guess we're screwed..."

"Yep. Blocked on all sides..."

Shining Saber's ale had gone tepid, but he chugged it before tossing back a handful of nuts and collapsing on the table in despair. Cohral smiled awkwardly and then polished off his own drink in a single gulp.

"So, what's the plan? Should we keep looking for the cause?" Cayna proposed.

Shining Saber squinted at her and shook his head miserably. "If an all-powerful Skill Master can't figure it out, there's no point in the rest of us trying."

"I agree. I'll just sadly think of my new name…as penance for this mishap…," Cohral muttered. His distant gaze stared at nothing in particular. It was as if he'd already accepted his fate and had shelved his feelings away in the back of his mind. Cayna hoped he wasn't going to explode.

She then stood. "Opus was watching you nearby during the match, so I'll see if he has any ideas."

"Yeah… Thanks…"

"Greaaaat…"

The mood was turning downright grim. "Later!" Cayna called as she left the tavern.

"What do you plan to do?" asked Kee, who had remained silent thus far, as she wove aimlessly through the crowd.

Before the conversation in the tavern, she had instructed him to speak up if anything caught his attention. Since he hadn't made a peep the entire time, Cayna had assumed he was equally clueless.

"My only real option is to look for Opus again and pick his brain about what happened."

Opus randomly disappeared right after the tourney ended on a sour note. Cayna also had questions about the Abandoned Capital, so she sent a telepathic message to the Double Rs to capture him immediately if they spotted him. Yet even after the festival had ended, Opus was nowhere to be found. The very real chance he had two hundred years' worth of safe houses scattered across the continent was a terrifying thought. That moron was always so damn hard to locate. According to Kee, Opus would most likely be a terrible servant who ignored Cayna's summons.

"Where in the world is he puttering around?"

All Cayna could manage in response to Kee's grumbling was a hollow laugh.

"Letter for youuuu!"

"Kuu?"

Out of nowhere, Kuu appeared in front of Cayna with a scrap of paper the size of a business card. Kuu wasn't one to reveal herself in a crowd, but at some point she had discovered a way to make herself visible only to Cayna. She still typically hid in Cayna's hair whenever they were out in public unless she had a good reason to pop out.

Kuu then handed the scrap of paper to Cayna. It read:

"The target has been apprehended.—Roxine"

"Huh? 'Apprehended'? Who?" Cayna froze, visibly confused.

"The person you were just talking about!" Kuu answered merrily.

"What? Roxine caught Opus? How?"

His depravity aside, Opus was still a limit-breaking Skill Master. Cayna didn't expect a level-550 maid would be able to capture him with such ease. She thought maybe Roxine could put up a good fight and slow him down, but the werecat had apparently pulled it off.

"You instructed her to capture him, did you not?"

"I didn't think it was even a possibility, considering the level difference, but it looks like she proved me wrong."

Cayna didn't know whether to feel shocked or proud. She entered a back alley, checked for prying eyes, then ran up the wall to the roof. After finding an unseen nook in the shadows, Cayna teleported to the remote village.

"Did you really capture Opus?!"

Cayna returned from Felskeilo in ten seconds flat and burst through the living room door. She gaped at the sight before her.

"Mommy Cayna?"

""Lady Cayna!""

"Welcome back, Lady Cayna."

Four people—Luka, Roxine, Roxilius, and Siren—sat around something tied to a chair. Covered in rope, it looked like a caterpillar and groaned "Mmph! Mmph!" as it wriggled in vain. The horns peeking out of its head indicated this was most likely Opus.

"Ah yes, that is indeed Master Opus," Siren said, confirming the caterpillar's identity.

"Uh, mind filling me in?" Cayna asked.

"I thought it best to wrap him up for now," Roxine confessed brazenly. She was treating her creator like an inanimate object.

The atmosphere was tense. A stern-faced Roxilius raised his hand, and Cayna bade him to speak.

"Right," he began. "First, Lady Luka distracted Sir Opus, then we took him down in an ambush."

"Uh, that's not what I meant by 'filling me in.'"

Their cold-blooded tactics gave Cayna a headache.

I bet Opus is, like, super pissed right now.

"Most likely. But you asked them to capture him, so this is your problem as well, correct?"

Yeah... Guess you're right.

Steeling herself against his inevitable wrath, Cayna was about to have Siren free Opus when the captured caterpillar deflated like a balloon. Strands of rope scattered around the chair.

"Oh," Cayna said, surprised.

""Ah!"" Roxine and Roxilius assumed battle positions.

"My pitiful master has withered away."

Siren dabbed her tears with her usual handkerchief, and Luka clung to Cayna.

"You're not sorry at all!" Opus yelled.

"Goodness, you're safe, Master. How unfortunate."

Opus was suddenly right behind them, and Siren offered him a bright smile. He had used the skills Rope Escape and Ninjutsu to break free. A vein in his temple throbbed, and he gnashed his teeth audibly. He stomped in frustration at his maid's attitude and then rounded on Cayna.

"What kind of deranged orders did you give your daughter and servants?!"

"Look, I'm sorry you got turned into a caterpillar, but you really shouldn't keep so many secrets."

"…What are you talking about?"

"The Abandoned Capital—"

"?!"

Opus fell silent and looked away as Cayna shot him a death glare.

"I knew it. You're up to something, aren't you? Spill it," she demanded.

"I had to set some things in motion first! I planned to tell you later…for the most part."

"So you were gonna leave me in the dark if those things never got in motion?"

"N-no, that's, uh, not it. I—I had my reasons. There were a lot of politics involved, y-you know?"

"Pfft."

"Huh?"

Watching Opus stand there frozen in a cold sweat made Cayna burst out in laughter. As far as she could tell, he'd never lost his cool like this before. It was refreshing.

"Yes, yes, good for you, pulling all those strings. You'll tell me everything now, right?"

"Y-yeah."

"'Kay. Let's get down to business."

While Roxilius and Roxine took care of Luka, the rest of the group (including Siren, who had been somewhat complicit in Opus's capture) moved their conversation to the Guardian room of Cayna's tower. Cayna and Opus sat at a table covered with a white linen cloth that Siren had prepared for tea. Kuu was unlikely to interrupt now that she was happily munching on a cookie.

"Hey, Master," the mural Guardian ventured, expression dubious.

"What's up?" Cayna replied with a cup of fragrant tea in hand.

"This ain't a lounge. You know that, right?"

"Of course. It's an ideal conference room where we can discuss things without fear of eavesdroppers."

Cayna's smile seemed pure but emanated a glacial iciness that left no room for argument. The mural Guardian grimaced, then closed its eyes and mouth—see no evil, speak no evil. It had apparently chosen to stay out of this discussion.

Opus shuddered as he observed this exchange. "So, even Guardians can't escape your iron fist? Scary."

"Don't be rude. We have a very normal Skill Master/Guardian relationship."

The way Opus saw it, these two were the very image of a lowly manservant and his queen, no matter how you sliced it. Still, he had no desire to be shot down like a green pheasant and let the matter drop.

"Okay, spit it out!" Cayna pressed.

"Can you wait two seconds before threatening me?!"

Opus got the sense that escaping those ropes changed nothing.

He turned to Siren for support, but she remained standing behind Cayna in silent solidarity.

His shoulders slumped. He was fully mentally checked out. "Instead of grilling me, why not just ask me like a normal person?"

"I've had a ton on my plate lately."

"I feel like we had plenty of opportunities to go over the most important points."

"The timing was just never right..."

Basically, she had forgotten and shamelessly hid the fact that it was entirely her own fault. Opus started to complain, but Siren clapped her hands, interrupting him.

"That's quite enough, you two. Our time will be wasted if you play around as usual."

"Yeah, you're right," said Cayna. "Thanks, Siren."

"It is my pleasure. This is a common occurrence, after all."

"Give me a break, Siren. Can't you muster up at least a shred of loyalty to me?"

"Whatever do you mean, Master Opus? I am simply treating you and Lady as equals...*precisely* as you commanded."

He may or may not have said something to that effect; Opus's memory was a bit fuzzy. A single bead of sweat dripped down his forehead.

"All that clandestine string-pulling makes you the villain here, does it not? Moreover, if you and Lady Cayna are indeed equals, isn't it only natural to share information?"

"Hmph..."

Opus was obviously dodging the issue. His orders to Siren had backfired and left him with little choice but to hem and haw.

Cayna smiled awkwardly as she listened to this conversation between master and servant. In a way, it seemed like the apple didn't fall far from the tree.

"Well, let's hear it already," she urged Opus.

"We won't get anywhere without a topic."

"Like I saaaaid, I wanna know about the Abandoned Capital. You already knew that!" Cayna protested, almost getting up out of her seat.

"Okay, okay. You don't have to yell over every little thing. I can hear you just fine." Opus crossed his arms and sighed. "But where do I even start...?"

Cayna, visibly doubtful, wondered whether it was really that complicated. Opus used Oscar—Roses Scatter with Beauty to cast a gloomy sky over his head. The dark clouds threatened to unleash a downpour at any moment.

"What gives? Are you trying to freak me out?"

"Well, I think you'll understand once you see it for yourself, but yes. You would have quickly come to the same realization if you did nothing, but I find the timing of your investigation odd."

"My timing...? I mainly looked into the Abandoned Capital because of Sahalashade. If I dig up enough information, she might be able to deal with it on her end, too."

"It's been forever since I heard that name. What is this about Sahana's pet, or whatever she is?"

Opus and Sahana fought like cats and dogs back in the day, so just speaking her name made him grimace.

"She's her Foster Child. Sahalashade was designated the queen of Otaloquess by a goddess or something. She's also my niece, apparently, but don't ask me how that works."

"The queen of Otaloquess? Your elite family tree keeps on expanding without you having to lift a finger..."

To be more precise, these "relatives" of hers were simply people in positions of power. It wasn't like Cayna had a hand in it; this outcome was completely out of her control. If anything, no one was more baffled by the showy lineup than Cayna herself.

"Look, let's save that for another day," said Cayna. "My goal right now is to investigate the Abandoned Capital and how it's hidden. There's probably an Isolation Barrier over the former Brown Kingdom, right? Still, that thing's defense and durability are through the roof. Also, isn't that where all these random quest monsters have been leaking from?"

"Most likely."

"'Most likely'? You mean you don't know?"

"That's right," Opus replied flatly.

Cayna's jaw dropped. It was a natural reaction, since Mr. One Step Ahead had just thrown her for a loop.

"Even though I hid away in that dungeon until recently, I still went out on occasion. I didn't really maintain that barrier, either. I've someone keeping an eye on the area for now, but they won't last much longer."

"What's going on over there?!"

"For now, it's protected by the strongest Isolation Barrier I can muster. And I added two or three extra layers just in case."

"Can something like that last for two hundred years?"

"It has, so the damage to the surrounding area is minimal. Although it seems to be gradually coming apart."

"Talk about irresponsible!"

Cayna had previously used Isolation Barriers for other purposes, and the effects weren't semipermanent. The barrier itself had preset defense and durability. Its defense changed according to the amount of MP added beyond the actual spell, and its endurance depended entirely on the caster's magic. You could even add keywords like *No evil shall pass.*

For example, what if Cayna cast an Isolation Barrier that possessed no defensive MP beyond the initial spell? Endurancewise, it could withstand even a full-on attack from Opus—though a second strike would finish the job. Of course, incessant pecking from the barrier's occupants would eventually shatter it as well.

There were only two ways to nullify a barrier: break it or, if you were the caster, cancel it. That was why the Isolation Barriers of left-over fortresses (former guild bases) couldn't be breached, and several remained intact.

"I called a summons to watch over the barrier," Opus explained. "When I first set it up, the game's service had just ended, and all *Leadale*'s functions—including you, me, and our sandbox—were transferred to this world. However, these random monsters that slipped in with the player avatars and active quests were a miscalculation."

"So you sealed them inside the Brown Kingdom?"

"Right. The Brown Kingdom had already fallen into ruin, so it was a convenient choice."

Cayna, the direct cause of the Brown Kingdom's ruin, slumped over. This was a sore spot that had made her the butt of many a joke.

"It felt like leaving the Abandoned Capital to its own devices wouldn't end well for this small population, so I chose several competent, skilled candidates to lead each nation. Mostly those with the Govern skill," Opus went on.

Players used Govern to develop regions under their control. If you had it equipped while transforming village hubs into fortresses in Offline Mode, you'd earn an extra boost. Still, Govern was yet another unfortunate skill that wasn't good for much else. There was talk that the same villages would appear online in future updates, although this never came to pass.

"Hang on—legend says a goddess chose people to lead each nation," Cayna said, recalling what Marelle had told her the day she'd awoken in Leadale. "Don't tell me you're into cross-dressing… What the heck?" She eyed Opus reproachfully.

"You couldn't pay me to do that, you fool! *She* addressed the public for me."

He swiftly shut Cayna down and gestured toward Siren, standing at attention behind her. The raven-haired elf maid smiled gently and nodded briefly. Cayna stared at her with grim suspicion.

"Yes, indeed! I dyed my hair a heavenly hue, cast an effect, and wore an Angel's Raiment, all at my master's behest..."

"Uwagh..."

Cayna's expression transformed into heartfelt sympathy. She got to her feet, turned to Siren, and brought her in a gentle embrace while patting her on the back. Even Kuu parted from her snack and stroked the maid's hair. Siren herself had no idea what was going on.

Overwhelmed by Cayna's kindness, Siren pulled a handkerchief from out of nowhere and dabbed at the corners of her eyes.

"There, there," said Cayna. "You had a rough time of it."

"*Sniff.* Lady Cayna..."

"Just think of it as a little bump in the road and put it out of your mind."

"Yes, I will. Thank you for your compassion."

"Hang in there, okay?"

"Okay..."

Lit up by a Stage Spotlight effect, the pair enacted a scene of an older friend comforting a young woman after a harrowing encounter with a dirty old man. Their height difference made it look more like a younger sister consoling her elder sister.

Meanwhile, Cayna, Siren, and Kuu gave Opus the stink eye.

"Wait—why are you all looking at me like that?!"

""""You're the worst."""

"Ngh..." Perhaps sensing he'd done something barbaric, Opus awkwardly averted his gaze.

Incidentally, an Angel's Raiment was a rare ornamental outfit imbued with Flight Magic. Like a certain celestial maiden of legend, the enchanting, long-sleeved kimono was encircled by a glittering sash and backlit by a divine halo. The see-through top was an unfortunate drawback, however, and female players considered it part of the despised Pervy Admins' Desire Series. Cayna knew exactly one person who could wear such an outfit with a straight face.

Siren was a beauty among beauties. Add in golden hair, an Angel's Raiment, and a heavenly aura, and anyone could mistake her for a goddess.

Skargo had spoken of this "deity" with such passion; now that Cayna knew the truth behind this world's legends, she felt a little bad for him. If anything, a lot of what he'd said was mere fantasy. It seemed that no man was exempt from putting certain women on a pedestal.

"At any rate, I think I'll keep this fact to myself," said Cayna. "Certain people might fall to pieces if their creation myth started coming apart…"

"Yes, the truth is often stranger than fiction," quipped the demon responsible for many strange truths.

Cayna didn't know if stomach medicine existed in this world, but she really wanted some in that moment.

From there, Opus briefly explained the time line of events after *Leadale* went offline. In short, there were three main points: the birth of the three nations, the imprisonment of the Event Monsters in the Abandoned Capital, and the handling of players stuck in this world.

Opus left most of the nation-rearing to Siren. She selected individuals who possessed the Govern skill from among Leadale's inhabitants and all the Foster Children, then divided the continent into north, central, and east sectors. This was around when the three nations were tasked with watching over the Abandoned Capital together. Surprisingly, only southern Otaloquess continued to uphold this duty two centuries later.

"The king of Felskeilo told me that Otaloquess is in charge of the Abandoned Capital…," said Cayna.

"You've been hobnobbing with the upper crust?" Opus sneered. "I'd always thought nobles were the bane of your existence."

"Unlike in the game, they're not all pompous jerks. Some definitely need to get off their high horses, though."

"Could it be that they lose interest in such obligations from generation to generation?" Siren lamented with a sigh. She appeared incapable of comprehending how anyone could have performed their duties so poorly.

However, Siren (the "goddess") was not to blame here. It was the descendants of these nation's leaders who were pathetic for shirking their responsibilities as time went on.

"Still, two centuries is at least four generations," said Cayna. "Kind of sloppy to forget your duties that quickly, don't you think?"

"Perhaps the original leaders died unexpectedly?" Siren offered. "That seems like a logical explanation if they passed away before sharing their knowledge with their descendants."

"Even if oral instruction was out of the question, they could have passed it on in different ways, like writing," said Opus. "Honestly, did the command of a goddess mean nothing to them?"

"It's a twisted telephone game!" Kuu shouted as she pointed to the sky and spouted nonsense. Siren deftly wiped off the crumbs around her mouth and clothes.

"A goddess *does* sounds pretty far-fetched," Cayna noted.

"Perhaps I was ill-suited to such a vital role?" said Siren.

"No, that's not what I meant. Besides Sahalashade, those who agreed to your orders were the ones with poor judgment. A power struggle is more important than duties from a goddess, right? This is why nobles are so—!"

"You're going ballistic for completely unrelated and groundless reasons. Have you forgiven them or not?"

Opus stared tiredly at Cayna as she ranted and raved. She gripped her head in consternation.

"Even if I talk to Skargo later, how the heck do I explain this…?"

Depending on the situation, Cayna thought it might be better to enter destruction mode and transform the Abandoned Capital into a crater. Warning about something set to disappear anyway would only waste precious energy.

"Oh," she started. "Not to change the subject, but the goddess religion and the Five Grand Dukes who serve the main gods or whatever—were those both part of your plan, too? Did you spread those ideas?"

"I didn't know this world's native beliefs, so I mostly just applied whatever was convenient."

"We should keep this from Skargo, too. He'll snap if I let it slip…"

After putting the issue of the remaining players on the back burner, the topic shifted to the Abandoned Capital.

"Who could've guessed our avatars would end up real?"

"Indeed," said Siren, agreeing with Cayna. "Master Opus did not expect it, either."

"I wonder how many there were back then…"

"They were temporarily frozen together, and I had to ignore them while I prepared my next steps."

After forcing the Event Monsters that had invaded every corner of the continent into the Abandoned Capital via a linked space and sequestering them within a three-layer Isolation Barrier, Opus had left the city entirely under the care of a suitable summons.

"You sure like to pass the buck. Why didn't you just round up the monsters and destroy the Abandoned Capital back then? Now it's a giant pain."

"You think I can fix everything in an instant? No man is an island."

"Lady Cayna, you say Master Opus has shirked his duties, but he checked on each area afterward to ensure all was well. Many players have awakened in the last fifty years—although he has curtailed his time outside to avoid potential encounters."

Some awakened players like Guan Yu had ventured beyond the Leadale continent, while others like humans and werecats had died of old age. More than a few had succumbed to illness or injury.

"Right," said Cayna. "You can't bounce back like in the game."

"Some never learn recovery skills to begin with," agreed Opus.

"Yep, totally. Cohral is one of 'em."

"Others don't use their money from the game and die destitute."

"Apparently, that was almost Tartarus's fate. The game's money is invisible, so not many people think to take it."

"That guy always has a comment ready. It wouldn't kill him to relax more."

Opus was referring to Tartarus's secondary account, Exis. Tartarus himself had decent common sense, and everyone in the guild considered him the resident snark who butted into every conversation. The situation had probably stressed him out, and thus Exis was born.

"So how do we get inside the Abandoned Capital?" Cayna asked Opus.

"Say *open sesame*."

"What? Seriously?"

"......"

A painful silence followed, and a chill ran down Cayna's spine.

Unable to meet her gaze, Opus nodded quietly. "......Yeah."

"Whaaaat?! Wait, are you dead serious right now?!"

"Yes, it's absolutely true."

"I doubted my own ears when I first heard it as well, but I promise it is neither a lie nor a joke," said Siren. "He assumed the people here did not know your world's culture."

Apparently, this password would open a three-layer Isolation Barrier.

"What if a player comes across it?!"

"I've already considered that possibility and established a major road system. Players don't leave the road often."

"Well, you're got a point there..."

Basic events and quests were usually held alongside the road back in the game, after all. This trend was used against them and allowed the Abandoned Capital to remain hidden. Incidentally, it was the First Skill Master Marvelia who pioneered the idea of wandering off the beaten path.

A summons still kept watch over the problematic capital itself.

"Ask the summons for more details," Opus insisted.

"It's *your* summons, right? Will it even listen to me? I'm sure everything will work out if you come along."

"I've still got some minor business here. Sorry, but you're on your own."

"My apologies, Lady Cayna. I cannot take my eyes off my master for nary a second, so I must ask you to handle the rest." Siren boldly whipped out a jangling metal chain.

Opus's face twitched. The maid had evidently established herself as a bigger deterrent than Cayna, which was a terrifying prospect.

"You've been acting fishy ever since we reunited, Opus," Cayna noted. "Don't I at least deserve an explanation? Or is it something you can't tell me?"

He had always been tight-lipped, but this was too much. He'd apparently been scheming in the background even before Cayna had awoken in this world. Figuring it was worth a shot, she asked what was going on so they could work together.

Opus looked conflicted. He fell silent for a moment before at last saying with defeat, "I've been quietly investigating the number of players."

"'The number of players'? You mean like how they've been dwindling for the past two hundred years?"

"No, the exact opposite. There are far more players than before. The initial headcount doesn't even compare."

"Why would it go up?! The game is long gone!"

"I found a large discrepancy between the number of players who disappeared when the game ended and the players who came to this world immediately afterward."

From what Opus had investigated, there had been only a few initial arrivals. More importantly, that number skyrocketed in the following decades.

"What the heck...?"

"Well, it's possible the game system in your soul began to stabilize. The avatars frozen in limbo between this world and the other until that point could have responded to this and dropped in rapid succession."

Cayna had no clue how the stabilization process worked, but it was apparently responsible for the seven-year difference between Shining Saber's arrival and Cohral's.

"So, this cryptic system inside me is to blame?" Cayna asked.

There was no way to verify such a claim, so she couldn't do anything about it. Others were probably still stuck in that void.

"No, your awakening has helped bring the rest here."

"Are there really that many players? I've barely seen any."

"That's because the majority are cautious. They're living in secret as regular people. Even Felskeilo's capital has a hidden yet significant player population."

"Geh?!"

Cayna's face paled at the mention of Felskeilo. Thanks to her involvement with Skargo *et al*, she was a household name there. Incidentally, any player would have known exactly what Cayna was up to when she planned that little act with the white whale tower. The previous glow of a job well done suddenly turned to mortification. Furthermore, there was a chance players might raid the whale tower in search of skills. Anxious to check up on this, Cayna started getting to her feet.

Opus stopped her with a wave of his hand. "There's nothing to worry about," he said. "Marvelia's massive whale tower must swallow the player first, so it would need enough space to move. The Guardian won't do anything without your permission, either. There are also local soldiers keeping a close eye on it. And the more devoutly religious citizens would never let anyone near the object of their worship."

"Hmm. Are you *sure* it'll be okay?"

"If you're so worried, have your Guardian contact it later."

"Oh yeah. I can do that?"

"Sure can, Master. Maybe take a minute or two to learn about my functions, would ya?" the mural quipped with one eye open.

After a proper check, the tiny cuckoo Guardian inside the whale had angrily replied, **"Don't"**—*ka-thunk*—**"act like"**—*ka-thunk*—**"we're pals!"**

"Most of our fellow players have social anxiety. Some even rely on their servants or sponge off others, so this will be an uphill battle," said Opus.

"I have questioned several about the situation," added Siren, "but everyone replied, *'People who can't just use the chat box are scary.'*"

"What, has dimension-hopping made them all skittish now?!"

One would assume a gentle-looking maid would make people more open to conversation. Maybe these shut-ins would feel more talkative with someone like Opus, whose wartime interviews had earned him a level of notoriety?

"So how do you propose we count the players? A national census?" said Cayna.

"No. Right now, I'm planning the first and last event in the sealed Brown Kingdom."

"Bwegh!"

Opus's confident declaration made Cayna do a spit take.

"An excellent idea, right?" he proclaimed proudly.

"Wouldn't it be more helpful to invite Gramps and crush the monsters as a Skill Master trio?"

"That's impossible."

He promptly shot down Cayna's proposed hostile takedown.

The Brown Kingdom's capital was relatively vast; if Cayna, Opus, and Hidden Ogre infiltrated one corner, monsters could escape in the opposite direction and send their search back to square one. There was no simple answer, and it was difficult to know what sort of environment two centuries in that sealed bubble had created. The monsters might have dramatically evolved, so their best bet was to slowly trap them within a ring of players. That was Opus's line of thinking.

"But every capital has a path to an underground dungeon, right?"

"They were destroyed early on by my master's servant," said Siren.

"This won't be a worst-case scenario like with the Black Kingdom. There isn't a Demon King lurking beneath the other six nations, after all."

"Yeah, I guess that's true." Cayna nodded vacantly as she remembered a past tragedy.

At the time, the Cream Cheese guildmaster had received reports about a Demon King in the Black Kingdom capital's underground dungeon. After goading everyone into defeating it as a test of their mettle, the guild merrily set off together in a rush of late-night excitement.

Cayna had only just become a Skill Master, something the other guild members hadn't yet achieved; the tables soon turned on them. The Demon King's ranged attacks wreaked so much devastation that the incident wasn't funny even in retrospect.

However, the outrageous reach of their foe's final attack pierced through the dungeon and straight up to the surface. As a result, every player and NPC in the Black Kingdom instantly died...and came back to life.

It wasn't even wartime, and anyone who had died in town immediately revived or respawned. The affected players' logs merely said *Died from aftershock of attack*, much to their confusion.

The amused Admins had reported the cause as "unknown," so the midnight massacre in the Black Kingdom capital quickly became one of the game's many enigmas—a sore point for the guild behind the incident.

"I'd rather not suffer that kind of guilt again...," groaned Cayna.

"Weren't you and Tartaroast the only ones who showed any real remorse?"

"Don't remind me!"

As Cayna recalled her absurd fellow guild members (Opus

included), she could only sigh. Still, their absence also struck her with melancholy.

"At any rate, will any of these wallflowers even show up to the event?"

"I would assume they'd think they'd be able to meet other players, but it's hard to know for certain until the actual day."

"I thought you were the great and powerful Opus."

"I'm not a mind reader."

A shadow seemed to fall over Opus's wry grin, but Cayna shook this feeling off.

"What's the matter?" he asked her.

"Nah, it's nothing! Anyhow, how can I help with this event quest of yours?"

"Make sure you participate. That's enough."

"R-right. Gotcha."

She enthusiastically volunteered but understood there was plenty going on behind the scenes that had nothing to do with her. At least he didn't say she wasn't needed. Cayna put a hand to her chest in relief.

"Me, Siren, and...my servants will suffice," Opus told her. "First, you should do as your daughter asked."

"How did you know about that...?"

"Snake—I mean, Kee—and I more or less exchange information. I need to know what's going on around you."

"What?! Kee?"

"Do not worry. I have only passed on information regarding the present quest."

"Geez! Be more careful with people's personal information!"

"I understand."

Cayna imagined Kee offering a stewardly bow, but his tendency to hand out details without permission would no doubt have her jumping at shadows later.

She'd definitely make Kee confess how much he had shared with Opus, but there wasn't really a way to punish someone inside her own head.

"Oh, what should I do about the barrier's watchdog?"

"Your daughter's request will grant you access, so just approach it."

"I'll be able to get back out, right?"

"Just don't rattle the barrier too much."

"Thanks for freaking me out!"

Opus's ominous warning sent chills down Cayna's spine, but she left the rest to him and teleported to the royal capital. After watching its Skill Master wave and leave them behind, the narrow-eyed mural let out a heavy sigh.

"Hey, mister. I heard the deets from your skeleton queen. Is my master gonna be okay?"

"I doubt even a team-up of every Limit Breaker in their heyday could rival her... Barring an unfortunate accident, that Snake will keep her safe."

To prepare for the worst, Opus had sent the details of his quest to every tower in operation. If, for example, the monsters inside the Brown Kingdom barrier were to stampede and either scatter over a wide area or target a specific point en masse, he planned to have the Guardian Towers erect a defensive wall. To accomplish this, Hidden Ogre was currently relocating his mobile tower to Otaloquess's southwest. Opus hoped the Dragon Palace, House of Murder and Malice, and Floating Sky Garden would be enough to encompass the Brown Kingdom's outermost limits.

"I don't like keepin' secrets from my master, y'know."

"She's likely to complain at the eleventh hour. Everything will work out as long as the players can eliminate them all."

"I sure hope we don't have to make an appearance. Hey, answer me."

"I'll see what I can d—"

Before Opus could finish his sentence, the Guardian whisked him outside. The grumpy wall Guardian heard his screams getting softer as he fell farther down the tower, but it didn't care.

"Hmph."

It gazed up at the vast blue sky with a heavy heart.

CHAPTER 2
A Meeting, a Request, Introductions, and a Revelation

Meanwhile, as Cayna bounced event ideas off Opus...

In the office of Felskeilo's High Priest, Mai-Mai and Skargo were having a meeting of their own. The Academy normally hosted an event around the same time as the tourney, but the schedule had been thrown out of whack, thanks to the wild duel between Shining Saber and Cohral.

"For some reason, I feel like we've had an inordinate number of surprises this year..."

"Perhaps it's because Mother has come out of hiding?"

"Watch your tongue, Mai-Mai. You'll pay dearly if you insinuate Mother Dear is to blame."

Mai-Mai sensed Cayna's shadow nearby whenever chaos broke out in the capital and accidentally spoke these thoughts aloud. Skargo had considered the same possibility, but the image of his mother's terrifying grin drained the color from his face and prompted him to admonish Mai-Mai.

Their present discussion revolved around staff recruitment even though, as an annual affair, the matter had been largely decided beforehand. It was only a formality, but the siblings rarely had the

chance to spend quality time together despite their close geographic proximity.

The school function in question was a survival course to be held outside the capital. There were several reasons why this coincided with the tourney.

First of all, since adventurers and other skilled individuals gathered in Felskeilo during the tourney, the threat of monsters around the capital decreased significantly. Lodgings also filled up fast during this time, so most adventurers booked an extended stay and paid for their room by taking on local monster requests. Their safety wasn't guaranteed, but it was easier to take out multiple enemies as a group.

In addition, excitement rose to a fever pitch around ten or so days prior to the tourney. The Academy took on a festive air, and classes were the last thing on anyone's minds. Eager to join the jamboree, volunteer students set up stalls on the school grounds for public enjoyment.

Aside from those tasked with supervision, the instructors had plenty of free time and were sent to oversee the survival course instead. Since the tourney had fizzled out like a balloon this year, a secondary festival was held to ease the citizens' disappointment. As far as the Academy was concerned, this just meant more time to party. The survival course was completely optional and included a liability waver that stated any loss of life during the survival course was not the responsibility of the Academy. It was, in other words, a last will and testament.

Even with the instructors and adventurers acting as minders, countless lives were lost each year due to unfortunate accidents. The Academy kept a watchful eye, but not everyone was accustomed to the great outdoors. Moreover, the adventurers doubled as both guards and guides, since most of the school's faculty was composed of reclusive researchers.

Mai-Mai was their headmistress and a former Imperial Mage. She could be counted on for firepower in a pinch, so leaving the capital was easier said than done. The training camp was primarily spearheaded by former adventurers and knights who had turned to teaching upon retirement.

"You have adequate guards, don't you?" Skargo asked.

"The princess will participate this year, so several Imperial Knights will accompany her. Our usual volunteer adventurers also made inquiries before registration even opened, and I've asked Mother to join as well."

"Do you intend to hire Mother Dear for a pittance? Curb your expectations, Mai-Mai."

"I always pay the adventurers a fair sum! Mother is among their number, so I'm certain she'll accept the same amount."

"Well, I suppose I can't argue with that…"

His sister's emphatic response overwhelmed Skargo. Indeed, their mother was not one to disregard her children's wishes.

"Those whom we accepted into the church last year are keen to participate. As former apprentices, they'll use their experiences to shepherd this year's initiates."

"I'm glad to hear your priests are growing up well, Brother."

"That is thanks to recent events. However, very few people still count as apprentices after all the activity over the past year, such as the attack on the capital."

The church sent healers to events to provide potions and the like, but their main objective was to cultivate their members. By assigning three or four apprentices to one veteran monk or nun, each novice could become more acclimated to working on the front lines. Aside from those who chose to embark on a pilgrimage, most in the church never left the capital. A survival course was therefore an excellent opportunity to train.

The tension from dealing with both a monstrous rampage and an ambush in a single year had undoubtedly accelerated the personal growth of all involved.

"Still, the Imperial Knights are going to escort the princess?" Skargo asked Mai-Mai.

"The knight captain has been busy since the tourney."

"Well, I must admit even I was dumbfounded."

When disaster struck the Battle Arena like a typhoon, even Skargo had to frown. His mother's unbelievable feats had convinced the High Priest he'd seen it all, but in that very moment, he felt there was still extraordinary talent hidden in this world.

The knight captain in question was responsible for the incident and had apparently been relieved of his post. He carried out assistant-type duties for the time being, which meant mountains of extra work for the co-captain. The knights as a whole were a jumbled mess.

After leaving Opus and flying off to Felskeilo, Cayna appeared in a waiting room of the cathedral via the whale Guardian.

Skargo had said the magic rhymestones would message him whenever someone (mainly Cayna) entered this room, and she steeled herself for his imminent arrival. However, the tall effect-happy weirdo never came. Suddenly suspicious, Cayna left the cathedral and headed for the Academy next door. The gatekeeper let her enter without argument and informed the headmistress.

"We dropped by at the last minute, but it was nice of them to give her a heads-up," said Cayna.

"Heads-up, heads-up!" Kuu parroted her and flitted happily through the air. The school building was mostly empty, so she wasn't too concerned about flying around in public.

"Oh, Miss Cayna!"

"Hi there, Lonti."

As Cayna walked down the hallway toward the headmistress's office, Lonti appeared in front of her with a bundle of papers. Kuu didn't bother hiding; she'd met Lonti a few times before (mostly when she was still invisible) and was likely used to her by now.

"You're still studying at a time like this?" Cayna asked Lonti.

"Huh? Ah! N-no, this is different!"

As Cayna eyed the documents with a smile, Lonti quickly explained herself. There was no reason to act so flustered, but she felt an odd urge to set the record straight.

"My grandfather told me I should learn how to run events for future reference. This time I've been put in charge of procuring supplies..."

"Whoa."

"I'm on my way to bring some materials to the school storehouse."

"Can you manage all this okay by yourself?"

"Yes, I have the help of a few students who also plan to become civil officials."

"I seeeee. That's fantastic," Cayna said with a smile, nodding repeatedly.

Lonti's face grew beet red. "R-right. Well then, are you visiting the headmistress?"

"Bingo. I got asked to be a guard for your school event."

"Both the princess and I will be very relieved if you're an escort!" Lonti broke into a wide grin.

Cayna picked up on a certain word in her response and pressed a hand to her forehead.

"I knew it," she replied. "I heard from Mai-Mai that Mye is going to participate, too. It's strange enough that you would enter, Lonti. She's your future queen. Is this really such a good idea?"

Lonti paused for a moment but soon determined it was safe to answer.

"Yes. It is reasonable for those unaware to be concerned, but royals must learn to stand on their own two feet."

"And that includes camping outside the city?"

"Y-yes, it does."

Lonti herself didn't sound entirely convinced. She looked away and didn't refute Cayna's exasperated comment.

"Huh... So it's like a custom?"

"Custom? Well, yes and no..."

Lonti put a hand to her cheek and looked briefly confused, but she panicked when she remembered the load in her arms.

"Ah, I'm sorry. Please excuse me, Miss Cayna."

"You've gotta deliver that, right? Sorry for holding you up."

"Not at all. I'll leave the escort matter to you. Please take care."

Lonti bowed several times before heading to the stairs. Cayna saw her off with a wave.

"Guess I've got no choice," she muttered, clenching her fist.

"You're gonna be a guard?" asked Kuu, already perched on Cayna's shoulder.

"Mai-Mai is counting on me, and how can I say no after what Lonti said?"

"Hmm." Kuu tilted her head curiously.

Cayna nodded. Her Skill Master name would be sullied if she didn't give 110 percent, but she wasn't too gung ho about the idea, either. Her work environment would be the straw that broke the camel's back.

She knocked on the headmistress's door.

"Come in!" Mai-Mai called from inside.

Cayna offered a cursory "Pardon me" before entering the room. Two other people, presumably faculty members, were present as well. Kuu sensed them and immediately hid behind Cayna. When her mother peeked out from behind the door, Mai-Mai paused their discussion. Her solemn expression melted into a puddle.

"Mother!"

""What?!""

"Ah, wait!"

Mai-Mai skirted around her desk like a ninja and ignored the stupefied instructors, lunging at Cayna with arms wide open for an embrace. Cayna intercepted this by seizing Mai-Mai's face in a vise-like grip.

"Agh-gah-gah-gah-gah?!"

""Headmistress?!""

"I *told* you not to cling to me in public!"

Mai-Mai crumpled as Cayna squeezed her face and broke into a lecture. Cayna then bowed to the two guests.

"You're so harsh, Mother!"

"And *you* mustn't ingratiate yourself at work," Cayna said, utterly fed up.

Surprisingly enough, the two faculty members wholeheartedly agreed. Their headmistress's frivolity had apparently put these two through the ringer as well. Mai-Mai urged them to resume their earlier conversation, but both insisted on some other time and turned to leave the office.

"Headmistress, please do not leave the room when you are finished."

Despite their smiles, this request was distinctly intimidating.

Exhausted, Cayna turned to her downtrodden daughter and asked, "What did you do *now*?" Once the door was closed, she scratched her cheek awkwardly. "Maybe this was a bad time…"

"Bad time, bad time! ♪"

"Not everything is a song, Kuu!"

Cayna glared at Kuu when she came out of hiding and broke out in singsong. The fairy ignored this with a cackle and landed on the recovered Mai-Mai's shoulder.

"Ouch, that hurt. Mother, please be a bit gentler."

"But I totally was. Otherwise your head would've been crushed like an apple."

"Eek!" Mai-Mai made a show of gripping her face and trembling.

"Your acting skills could use some work."

Mai-Mai then offered Cayna a seat on the sofa. She sat across from her.

"Thank you for coming, Mother."

"Why didn't you act like this from the get-go?"

"You might call it a conditioned reflex or perhaps my love for you…"

"Well, at least you don't sparkle like Skargo."

Her adult children (Kartatz excluded) really needed to find new love languages. The mental gymnastics made Cayna let out a heavy sigh.

"So were you able to look into that thing you mentioned?" Mai-Mai asked.

"Yeah, I guess. The situation only went downhill from there, though."

"Is there another issue in Felskeilo?"

"No, no, this is personal business. I'm fine with the escort job, but I've got a few conditions."

"Conditions? Can you only accept the job for a day or so?"

"Something like that. I'm free for now, so I can tag along on an outdoor excursion for two or three nights. However, I'd like permission to step away for a minute if necessary."

Mai-Mai closed her eyes and contemplated for a moment. Then she nodded. "If you can find a replacement, I believe we can accommodate you. I will inform the assigned faculty members, but please speak with the princess yourself."

"You're okay with it?!"

Although Cayna had brought it up, she didn't expect her daughter to readily agree.

"I don't grant most adventurers such freedom, since they only wish to slack off, but I will make an exception for you, Mother. After all, you are not one to leave a job undone. You *do* have a good reason, yes?"

"Oh, totally! It could even change the fate of the continent! Yeah!"

As Cayna quickly explained herself, Mai-Mai frowned.

"The fate of the continent! Is our situation so dire?! Shouldn't that take priority?!"

As far as Mai-Mai was concerned, no one was stronger than Cayna. If such a heavyweight was claiming something could "change fate," one could only imagine it was a heart-pounding race against time to prevent some unprecedented disaster from befalling this world.

Mai-Mai leaned forward, and Cayna took hold of her shoulders.

"I'm saying we'll deal with it when the time comes," she told Mai-Mai.

"By 'we,' do you mean that someone else is involved?"

"To be fair, Opus is the one running the show. I'm free until he gives the signal."

"Uncle Opus…? Forgive me for prying, then."

Mai-Mai quickly backed off. She clearly had great faith in Opus, which bothered Cayna to no end.

Sure, Cayna had introduced Mai-Mai to him as "your father's older brother," but Mai-Mai was way too trusting of this person she'd only just met.

"Are you certain it is not simply because he has a calm, collected appearance and radiates a different sense of security?"

Kee, are you calling me childish?

"Are you not a literal seventeen-year-old girl?"

Nghhhh. I hate when I can't say anything back...

"M-Mother?"

Cayna's self-awareness had been cranked up to eleven. Mai-Mai noticed her sudden visible frustration and ducked for cover, fearing her mother's wrath, but there was no need.

"Venting one's anger is improper."

Cayna then realized Mai-Mai was afraid. She took a small breath and suppressed her irritation.

"Sorry about that, Mai-Mai."

"What was that all about, Mother?"

"Nothing, I was just a teensy bit jealous of Opus, since you seem oddly attached to him... A-anyway, forget about that. You basically want me to shadow Mye, right?"

"Yes, please remain by princess's side as much as possible. If you have time, please check on the other students as well."

"But other adventurers will join, too, right? Can't you leave the rest to them?"

"There will be two adventurer parties and several Imperial Knights."

"'Imperial Knights'? Those don't sound like regular knights. Royals really are another breed."

Mai-Mai's expression soured at this, and Cayna questioned her curiously. However, the answer wasn't at all what she'd expected.

"The knight captain is currently busy atoning for his actions, so the knights as a whole have been overwhelmed. A last-minute decision was made to entrust this task to the Imperial Knights. Ah, these knights will be female, so there is no need for decorum."

"I heard the adventurers and knights have always butted heads, thanks to Shining Saber."

"My apologies, Mother. I'm afraid I don't have many details on the subject."

Apparently, even the Academy headmistress wasn't in the loop. Cayna's only information came from the vague hearsay she'd picked up in the Adventurers Guild when she'd first become an adventurer. Unbeknownst to Cayna, Shining Saber had cleaned up his act after getting pushed around by Arbiter. Thanks to this, the relationship between the knights and adventurers was on the mend.

"In any case, what's the highest level of these students who need guarding?"

"'The highest level'…? Compared to you, anyone else is no more than a baby chick."

"No, I mean what level of monster can they safely take on?"

For some reason, Cayna smiled as she recalled the times she would watch over grinding newbies from behind. Just as she wondered if it was something that innocent, Mai-Mai heaved a grand sigh.

"This isn't combat training. It's a camping trip! Over half of the participants are non-combatants, so we'd like the adventurers to clear out any danger."

"Ah, it's *that* kind of training. Gotcha. I've been thinking it was a monster-hunting course this whole time. You should've said so to begin with, Mai-Mai."

"*Sigh.* I apologize for the oversight, so please lend us a hand."

"Leave it to me! I'll return Mye and Lonti without a scratch on 'em!"

"…I'm more nervous than ever."

"Whyyy?!" Cayna moaned when Mai-Mai held her head in her hands.

"Will we leave early in the morning?" Cayna then asked.

"That is still up in the air. I believe they'll gather throughout the morning and arrive at camp before evening. Probably…"

"You're sure playing things fast and loose."

"That's because there are nobles involved. You don't have to worry about keeping a strict schedule during the course itself. Please ask the adventurers who will be traveling with you for more details. I'm sure you'll find them easier to talk to."

Cayna had assumed they'd leave at the crack of dawn, so Mai-Mai's response was a bit of a letdown. Apparently, the school trip basics in Cayna's old world didn't apply here.

On the way out, Mai-Mai instructed Cayna to formally accept the Academy's request at the Adventurers Guild. After walking across the river toward her destination, Cayna greeted the fishermen mending their nets along the bank and realized something.

"I get it now. Are players hiding from me because I stick out like a sore thumb?"

"It is very likely. They're not afraid of being exposed as players but rather have no desire to be lumped together."

"I guess they haven't accepted their avatars as part of themselves yet? At any rate, now we know why everyone's been keeping their distance."

Cayna thought maybe Cohral or Shining Saber knew of any hidden players, but she soon came to the conclusion that they were likely just as clueless. After all, neither had spoken a word about it so far.

"Actually, I bet they know and just decided to leave people alone."

"Maybe they think you might go chargin' in!" Kuu chirped merrily as she poked her head out from Cayna's hair.

Even Cayna didn't have the guts to visit a random player's home.

"I'd be shocked if they took me for a troublemaker like that."

She and Kuu arrived at the Adventurers Guild. When Cayna looked around and failed to see Cohral or any other familiar face, she headed over to the counter.

Almana had recently become Cayna's go-to employee, and she quickly processed the Academy's request.

"There. You're all ready to go."

"Thanks, Almana."

"Miss Cayna, were you asked to do this job personally since your daughter is the headmistress?"

"Yep. They practically begged me to do it."

It was a bit of an exaggeration, but Cayna didn't feel like going into detail and tried a bit of humor instead. The joke didn't land, though; the guild staff twitched and replied, "Ha-ha-ha... I see," with hollow laughter.

"Come to think of it," said Cayna, "I didn't even ask where this thing is. Do you know the location and when I should get there?"

"It's two days from now in front of the western gate," Almana told her. "You ought to ask about those details ahead of time."

"Right. Sorry."

Cayna offered Almana a sincere apology for annoying her.

The guild had recruited earth mages to fill in the giant hole carved out during the earlier attack, so the road was once again open to traffic.

"If you meet other adventurers, I think you should use communication to create a good first impression," Almana advised Cayna. "Strong relationships are built on solid foundations."

"Ohhh. Yes, yes, I see."

Cayna had mostly formed parties with her fellow guild members and pretty much gone solo in the last days of the game, so she could respect that sort of advice. Her automatic secretary (Kee) took note of Almana's comments and filed them away for future encounters.

After exiting the Adventurers Guild, Cayna realized the supplies in her Item Box were dwindling and headed to the market to buy staples like fresh meat and vegetables.

"Phew, that was a close one. I always hand over any food to Cie after I go grocery shopping, so there was hardly anything left."

"We never use it!"

"Your food's in there, too, Kuu... Anyway, what about you? There'll be lots of strangers at this event, but do you want to come along?"

"Hmm..."

Although the fairy boldly flitted around the remote village, she wasn't used to people. If Kuu went on this mission, she'd probably have to stay in Cayna's hair the entire time.

"Would you like to watch the house with Lu?"

"What? Nooooo!"

Cayna had proposed the idea so Luka could keep Kuu company, but the fairy started throwing a fit in midair. She was like a tantruming toddler.

"No! No! No! No!"

"Right..." Cayna was at a complete loss.

Kuu grabbed her hair and yanked it back and forth, screaming "Nooo! Nooo!"

"Ow, ow, ow, ow?! I got it! I understand, okay?! Ouch! You can come along, so stop pulling my hair already!"

As soon as the pain forced Cayna to backtrack, Kuu did a complete 180. Her tears dried in an instant, and she broke into a huge smile.

"Yippee!"

"Hmm. Is the subsystem ineffective on its own? Is that why you roam around the village alone but stick to me like glue anywhere else?"

Cayna watched Kuu curiously as the fairy hopped up and down and cheered.

Just to be safe, Cayna later informed Opus of her plans: She'd go to that thing, check on the barrier along the way, and be done in three days. It was all a bit thrown together but better than nothing. In any case, the point was to make sure the Abandoned Capital didn't interrupt her escort assignment.

"I should've asked Mai-Mai for a trip itinerary," said Cayna.

"Don't expect the Academy to provide the kinds of materials that schools in our previous world would," Opus replied.

"Looks like I'll have to take the brunt of the attack if any high-level monsters pop out."

"Well, I'll show up unannounced if necessary."

"Wouldn't be the first time you've thrown a wrench in my plans."

"Really? I wasn't aware."

"You're not foolin' anyone."

Back in the Game Era, Opus was constantly interrupting Cayna's plans, whether she was practicing a dry run for a secret scheme to invade a large army with her small party or laying traps in enemy territory before the next war. Now that she thought about it, absolutely no good came out of it.

"Do-do-do-doooo! ♪ Da-da-do-da-do-dooo! ♪"

Despite an unpleasant stroll down memory lane, the sky was blue and put some pep in her step. Captivated by the fine weather, Cayna's mood lightened. She felt the sudden urge to break into a run.

"Oh yeah, I used to hear kids running around the hospital courtyard whenever it was nice outside and wonder, *'What's so fun out there?'* Now I see what all the fuss was about."

Cayna quietly sighed as she recalled the days she spent watching the sun dye the wall of her hospital room from white to yellow. A friendly younger girl who would come to play with her used to ask, *"You can come outside, too, right?"* She'd simply reply, *"Maybe one of these days."*

However, she had been paralyzed from the neck down, and every ounce of muscle had shriveled from her limbs. Despite the full life ahead of her, rehabilitation was a distant dream if she couldn't even move. Empty promises only went so far.

It was more or less possible to heal the entire body, thanks to advancements in regenerative medicine, although the costs were astronomical. Her uncle had suggested they give it a try, but Cayna had no intention of burdening him with that kind of debt, nor did she ever expect to regain full mobility. Considering the places she'd been since then and her current situation, life was truly unpredictable.

"Guess this crowd is feeling pretty upbeat, too."

Cayna took a good look around her. Even Felskeilo's western shopping district felt different than usual with all the people milling about. Rows of vendors dotted the roadside, and passersby in search of food or rare goods took turns poking their heads in.

The capital's main road wasn't so bad, but there wasn't even a cobbled path in this area. The well-trampled ground was uneven and a bit awkward. Since Cayna was short and likely to be buffeted in the sea of people, every step was a chore.

"We just need to get a little higher."

Certain she'd fare somewhat better on the rooftops, Cayna slipped into a narrow alley and away from the masses. There was no escaping the public eye, so she would also need Invisibility to cross the buildings.

But traversing a side street was tricky for a different reason altogether.

Vagabonds in tattered rags leaned against the walls, and a huddle of orphans looked up at Cayna with piercing eyes. Others stared blankly at the sky and muttered nonsense.

Sometimes life throws you a curveball. In this case, she encountered some unneeded ruckus when a sketchy clandestine group (or not-so-clandestine, since the Covert spell was useless against Cayna's Passive Skill ESP) dressed in all black crossed her path.

"Whoa, shady people at ten o'clock!" she yelled.

"Ngh! Foul wench!" the shadowy gang's leader cried. "How could the likes of you detect us?!"

"Uh, what period drama did you walk out of?"

He drew his short sword and prepared for battle. Behind him, the rest of his group likewise wielded their chain-sickles and shurikens. Cayna wasn't really sure what they expected to accomplish. The leader mistook Cayna for a threat and struck without warning.

"We can't let her report us! Everyone, attack!"

Having decided the narrow street was inconvenient, Cayna clung to the wall like a spider. Then, channeling her inner flying squirrel, she attacked to the left and right from above. Players higher than level 500 used to come at her during wartime in the Game Era, so these guys were small fries by comparison.

Magic Skill: Electric Paralysis Net Zam Parat: Ready Set

"Time to zap some bugs."

"""Gweh?!"""

Cayna went easy on them, of course. A web of paralyzing lightning shot from every direction, and flickering yellow sparks lit up the corner of the back street as each shadowy figure fell to the ground in convulsions. Like mosquitoes doused in repellant, the poor ruffians didn't have a single member left standing. They were a bit burnt and scraped up, but at least they were alive. Cayna kept her would-be attackers on the ground with a gravity spell and prepared to call any soldier on patrol.

However, when Kuu gleefully pointed and announced that she'd done the honors, Cayna instead found a red arrow floating directly toward them from the main road. When several curious onlookers sneaked a peek, Cayna said she had captured a suspicious group and asked them to call the guards, which they promptly did. She didn't know what to do about the people who saw her and said, "Oh, you're that young lady who walked across the river."

The guards rushed to the scene, and Cayna showed them her registration ID before handing over the sketchy men. Several guards had either recognized Cayna or surmised what happened and didn't keep her very long.

"We'll send you a reward via the Adventurers Guild," one guard told her.

"Thank you for upholding the peace," said another.

Their gratitude made Cayna blush, but she bowed and hurried to the meet-up location.

"Why'd I have to run into trouble *now*?"

"Wouldn't you say this is a common occurrence?"

"I don't remember turning into a rabble-rouser..."

Cayna was getting sick of Kee's usual biting commentary. If incidents like this kept happening, she might as well stick to the crowded main road.

Cayna neared the public square by the western gate and finally managed to escape the crowds. She loosened up her shoulders, which had been bumped and jostled by various items and people.

"Phew..." She sighed. "Darn, why didn't I just hop on the rooftops regardless of who saw?"

Beyond the western gate, there was a cluster of several Academy students. Noon was still hours away, and Cayna watched everyone chat with the instructors. A group of fully equipped adventurers stood a short distance away from them.

Cayna showed the gatekeeper her registration. Once the departure procedures were complete, she waved to a familiar face and walked over.

"Hey there, Cohral. Short time no see!"

"Huh, Cayna? You're coming, too? Guess we've got nothing to worry about now."

"I'm only one person, y'know. Don't get too comfortable."

Besides, Cayna was mainly the princess's chaperone. It wasn't that she *couldn't* protect the other students, but in truth, she wanted to avoid unleashing her (largely destructive) powers on the front lines. That kind of damage was nothing to sneeze at.

Members of Cohral's adventurer party, the Armor of Victory, also greeted her.

"Miss Cayna is joining us?"

"Yeah. It was a personal request from her daughter, who runs the Academy."

"Wow, that sounds rough." Their party leader—a male mage—smirked.

Cayna couldn't help but wonder what adventurers thought of Mai-Mai. She got the impression from this trio's reactions that the Academy headmistress wasn't their cup of tea, although she'd probably need to take a survey to be totally sure.

The next group to shake Cayna's hand was a second adventurer party known as the Swift Horses. There were two men and two women who appeared to be in their thirties, and they specialized in exploring and scouting.

"It's a pleasure to meet you, Lady River-Crosser."

"Lady River-what…?!"

Cayna froze as they shook hands. Apparently, that nickname was well-known in adventurer circles.

Cohral reflexively spluttered, his shoulders trembling in silent laughter. Cayna shot him a death glare, and he crumpled when a comrade jabbed him in the side.

The male leader of the Swift Horses didn't get away scot-free, however. The two women in his party yelled "Hey!" and smacked him.

"Sorry, sorry," he said. "There are lot of rumors floatin' around about you, like how you're the High Priest's mother and you saved the city from a monster invasion. I wasn't sure how to approach you."

"Not calling her River-Crosser would be a good start!"

"Show a little sensitivity, Jild!"

His female comrades scolded him on Cayna's behalf.

"Umm...?" said Cayna.

"Oh, sorry. I'll watch my mouth next time. Let me start over. I'm Jild, leader of the Swift Horses. I know this is just a quick trip, but we're glad to have you."

The two women behind him waved briefly and winked.

"Hi, I'm Cayna. It's nice to meet you."

Although shocked at first, Cayna put Jild's comment behind her and told him she wasn't offended. After all, he wasn't wrong about her antics. She'd take River-Crosser over Silver Ring Witch any day.

Cayna breathed a sigh of relief, and Cohral lightly tapped her shoulder.

"Hey there, Lady River-Crosser. How you feelin'?"

"I'm starting to think the students would be a lot better off with the Supreme Swordsman instead of li'l old me."

"Gweh..."

She hit a nerve. This time it was Cohral who fell into bitter silence. Cayna smirked, and Cohral raised both hands in surrender.

"Didn't anyone ever teach you to treat others the way you'd want to be treated?" she asked him.

"Look, I'm sorry. Forgive me, would ya?"

"Is now a good time?" Jild ventured as his party approached.

Cohral quickly took the hint and called over his own party.

"What's up?"

"I'd like to more or less determine our rotation schedule while we still can. Keeping guard will be our top priority once we arrive, so there won't be time to talk."

"Yes, that's true," Cohral replied. "We need to make sure we're on the same page, since Cayna will be with us. We can keep the same arrangements as last time if that works for you."

The Armor of Victory and the Swift Horses had apparently been working together for a while. Thinking she should probably clarify her own mission first, Cayna meekly raised one hand.

"Just FYI, I'm only here to protect one person in particular."

"Right, we heard. One of those royals lost her mind and decided to join in. Anyway, can you take the night shift?"

"Jild, that kind of talk is treasonous," one of his female party members chided.

"Let's keep it between us, then," he said, waving apologetically. "No harm, no foul."

The Armor of Victory members, who had heard every word, nodded wryly. Not a big fan of royals herself, Cayna also played dumb.

"I should first ask Mye—I mean, the person I'm escorting, right?" she asked.

"...You two know each other?"

"She's sort of a friend, I guess? Also, I doubt your treasonous comment just now would upset her."

Cayna's speculation made everyone put a hand to their chests in relief. Granted, she'd never seen Myleene get angry. Therefore, she was really just guessing.

"At any rate, I can summon something if you need a night guard."

""""...What?"""""

Cayna's casual offer produced a wave of question marks over the heads of everyone present, except for one. Unlike the rest of the group, Cayna had no idea that the word *summon* didn't come up in normal conversation.

"Hold it, hold it! Whatever you summon is gonna be insane!" shouted Cohral, the only person who understood the gravity of the situation. He stopped Cayna (who looked mystified by their reactions) in her tracks, then briefly pulled her aside and whispered in her ear. "No one just whips out a summons. Try to control yourself."

"Really? But I've gotta step out for a bit while we're on the road and thought I'd ask it to protect Mye for me."

"Why do you have to leave halfway?"

"The Brown Kingdom barrier is nearby, and it seems to be deteriorating. I want to go check up on it— Oops. Was I not supposed to say that?"

Opus was partly to blame, since he hadn't sworn her to silence, but Cayna had dropped her guard and let a few facts accidentally slip because Cohral was a fellow player. In any case, she assumed Cohral would find out sooner or later, thanks to Opus's planned event, and she gave up trying to backpedal.

Cohral, meanwhile, was dumbstruck. He gasped at this momentous revelation, and his face went pale. He'd known about the barrier around the Brown Kingdom but had never heard any news about it failing. The uncertain situation inside the Abandoned Capital made him even more anxious.

"D-don't leak critical info like that!"

"My bad. We were talking and it just slipped out."

"You're not sorry at all!"

"Hey, you would've found out eventually. Everything's gonna work out, so no worries."

"You're being *way* too optimistic here! Seriously, this is *exactly* why I can't deal with Limit Breakers!"

"Relax! It's all good. Look, everyone's staring at us. We'd better head back."

Their private conversation had turned into a full-blown argument, and the spotlight was suddenly on them. Turning on the charm, Cayna and Cohral waved off the circle of onlookers with "Nothing to see here!" and then returned to Jild and the others.

"That sounded like a pretty intense one-on-one," said Jild.

"Not at all. I was hoping to drill some common sense into her, but no luck, I'm afraid," Cohral replied with disappointment as he patted Cayna's head.

Hollow laughter rose from his audience.

"She *is* Lady River-Crosser, after all."

"Yep. She cut right across it."

"Nothing sensible about walking on water, that's for sure. Any adventurer in Felskeilo could tell you that."

"Yeah, no need to remind us."

Everyone unanimously agreed that Cayna's behavior was absurd.

She curled up on the ground in defeat. *I told you so,* Cohral's smug expression seemed to say. He continued patting her head with a falcon-like grip.

"Gyah!" she yelled. "My hair's getting all messed up!"

The crowd burst into hysterics. Cohral thought Cayna's lack of common sense was no laughing matter, but he didn't say another word. Everyone would realize their folly whether they liked it or not.

As for the night shift, it was decided they would discuss it with the Imperial Knights, since they were also coming as escorts.

"Do we really need Cayna if the Imperial Knights are here?" Cohral muttered.

"There is no safer place than by Mother's side!" a voice responded from behind Cayna.

"Mai-Maiii?!"

"Eeee! Mother! It's been *days*!"

A harried cry escaped Cayna's throat when she turned around and saw the person standing there. The sunny Academy headmistress Mai-Mai Harvey squeezed her tight, and suddenly the students, teachers, adventurers, and even the gatekeeper stared in shock at what looked like a tearful reunion between sisters.

"Just hold your horses. A hug after only a few days loses all impact."

"But Motherrrr!"

Cayna peeled off Mai-Mai through sheer force as every last shred of energy drained from her expression.

"Umm, Headmistress?"

"Yes, I'm coming."

Although she was reluctant at first and wriggled in anguish, Mai-Mai answered her instructors' calls. In a split second, she was like a different person. Her expression turned serious, and she put on a mask of flawless elegance and professionalism. Adventurers and students alike had to rub their eyes and do a double take.

"Agh, geeeez!"

Cayna couldn't afford to relax now that this little surprise had shown up out of nowhere. She slumped over once more. Mai-Mai didn't mind her slack-jawed audience at all. Cayna could've learned a thing or two from that bold attitude but lacked the gumption.

"That one of your foster kids?" Cohral asked.

"Yeaaah. You probably know by now, but Mai-Mai's my daughter."

"Bit late to take back that relationship, huh?"

"…You don't have to spell it out."

As much as Cayna wanted to mourn her luck, Mai-Mai was her

own creation. Still, it wasn't inconceivable to think she'd purposefully made her daughter a bit of a mommy's girl.

Two more people made eye contact with Cayna and rushed over to her.

"It's been a while, Cayna!"

"Good morning, Cayna."

Upon closer inspection, the two young ladies were accompanied by a small, single-horse carriage and three female knights in full armor. Cayna used Search to check the knights' stats and felt an odd sensation. She tilted her head curiously.

"What's wrong, Cayna?"

"Oh, nothing. Nothing at all. Right—morning, Lonti. Long time no see, Mye."

"Good morning," said Lonti.

"It's been quite a while," said Myleene, who offered an exceptionally deep bow.

Cayna met this with a strained smile. The princess was being far too modest for royalty; Cayna was extremely concerned for the future.

"Thank you for accepting my request," Myleene told her.

"I was pretty surprised. I didn't have much choice, though, since I said I'd help as long as there was a reward involved," Cayna replied apathetically with a wag of her finger.

Myleene puffed out her cheeks. "You could have refused if you were busy..."

"No way. I could never just leave you to the elements. I'll protect you with everything I've got!" Cayna declared with boundless pride.

Myleene and Lonti looked worried.

"Um, Cayna," Myleene began. "There will be a lot of people around this time, so please don't summon your White Dragon again."

"Nor the giant wolves either, if possible...," Lonti added.

"No worries! Just leave everything to me. I'll stay well within the realm of reason!" Cayna thumped her chest to emphasize this loose promise.

The girls were visibly aghast.

""You, reasonable??""

They recalled the many outlandish feats Cayna had performed and failed to come up with a less dubious response. The two girls let out heavy sighs and prayed this outing would conclude without incident. They couldn't do much more than offer the heavens a tiny prayer.

"...At any rate, will you be okay, Lonti? Want me to carry that?" Cayna pointed to Lonti's massive backpack.

Myleene had on a traveling cloak and carried a wand. She wore light leather armor, and there was a rapier and small pouch at her side.

Lonti, on the other hand, carried enough equipment for a snowy mountain expedition. She was the daughter of a marquis, yet she was dressed like a porter.

"Oh, I'll be fine. This backpack has weight-reduction attributes."

"Seriously? It must be a national treasure."

"Heh-heh. This is a first-rate product my grandfather found during his travels in his youth."

"Agaido was an adventurer, too?! What's with these nobles?!"

The students watched in shock as Cayna engaged in friendly banter with the princess and a noble lady. They were well aware of Myleene's and Lonti's social standing and couldn't hide their surprise that an adventurer both knew the princess and spoke to her with such familiarity.

"My, I thought princesses rode in fancy carriages and had a dozen attendants!"

"They travel in style on occasion, yes, but the forest is no place for such transportation, is it?"

"Your bottom would never stop hurting if you took a carriage on that kind of terrain."

"So that's the issue here…"

Cayna had heard enough aristocratic opinions for one day.

One of the female Imperial Knights stepped in and said, "We shall serve as the princess's ladies-in-waiting for the time being. I assure you she will want for nothing."

"Right," Cayna replied. "Please talk to the adventurers about night patrol later as well."

"Will do, although it's unlikely our schedules will line up, since the three of us alternate in shifts."

"I don't think you can team up with them like that, but it'll all work out regardless. I'll get a night watch, too."

"A…night watch?"

The Imperial Knights were visibly confused, but Myleene and Lonti slightly grimaced.

"Cayna? Please try your best not to cause trouble for everyone."

"Hey, no worries. I'll show you later, so don't knock it just yet."

"Is this really going to work out, I wonder?"

Unfathomable anxiety struck the two girls as Cayna brimmed with confidence.

Meanwhile, Mai-Mai had finished her basic prep meeting with the faculty. Now standing before the students, she clapped to grab their attention for the morning assembly.

"All righty, everyone! Let's go over some final tips before you start training!"

"Is this in the headmaster job description?" Cayna pondered.

"Lady Mai-Mai is a marvelous leader," Myleene replied.

Mai-Mai explained each point to the attentive students as if she was a close friend. As Cayna considered what it meant to be a true leader, Myleene nodded in satisfaction.

"Still, is this really everyone…?"

Cayna looked around and saw there were only sixty participants in this survival boot camp. To be more precise, thirty-five (including Myleene and Lonti) were Academy students who all wore either blue or green robes. There were about eight instructors dressed in brown robes and cloaks. One battle veteran priest and four monks sent by the church were also present, in addition to three Imperial Knights. There were four adventurers in the Swift Horses party and five in the Armor of Victory. And finally, Cayna had come alone.

Three covered wagons driven by capable students would hold their camp luggage and double as medical rooms in the event of an emergency. The rest had to walk to the training ground.

"That is all! Please be careful and continue to grow step by step!"

Mai-Mai concluded her cautious yet inspirational morning assembly, then gathered the staff together for one final check. Afterward, a faculty member who acted as general supervisor ordered everyone to head out.

Mai-Mai later pattered over to the tail end where Cayna and the others waited to move.

"Thank you again for all your help, Mother," she said with a wink.

"Mai-Mai, there are some things even I'm not capable of. You know that, right?"

"Yes, but your very presence is so reassuring!"

"Well, I'll do whatever I can. Even if worse comes to worst and I gotta use Revival Magic."

"Stop right there!"

"Don't even think about it, idiot!"

As soon as Cayna proudly hinted at invoking an art lost to the modern world, Mai-Mai and Cohral protested in unison. Mai-Mai shot her mother a reproachful look.

"I'm joking," Cayna insisted with a smirk.

Mai-Mai, however, felt a pang of fear.

"We're not going off the beaten path just yet, right?" Cayna asked Lonti.

"Yes. In addition to the Academy, the Adventurers Guild also uses this road for their own exercises."

"Gotcha."

Cayna had assumed they'd continue down the main road, but the survivalists suddenly veered out of the western gate and entered the forest to the southwest.

As Lonti explained, it was a well-trodden road that didn't present too many challenges. Since a high elf like Cayna enjoyed the blessings of the forest, the bumpy terrain was even easier for her than for most.

She'd heard that the spacious campground the Academy used each year was over a half day's walk from the capital. Despite such close proximity, one couldn't be too careful, since visibility in the forest was limited. There had been many vicious monster attacks in the past, so the adventurers and every able-bodied instructor formed a tight, defensive circle. This tense atmosphere weighed heavily on the students.

The Swift Horses handled security and reconnaissance at the forefront, while the Armor of Victory stayed in the center and stood poised to jump into battle at any moment.

The only relaxation to be found was in the very back, where Cayna protected Myleene and the others. The three Imperial Knights were present as well, but anyone would agree they seemed more like eye candy as opposed to a combat unit. This wasn't an issue, since the women actually *could* fight, but it certainly didn't look that way.

Cayna promptly sent three Wind Spirits into the area and cast a surveillance net wider than anyone else's. As a high elf, she'd be directly informed by the forest of any threats lurking nearby. Incidentally, Kee's incredible range vastly outmatched even a player's skills. If trouble did find the students, the Wind Spirits would deal with it first. One might call it a safety lineup.

Still, there was a flip side; Cohral lost his cool when he learned about Cayna's actions after the fact and shouted, "You're gonna hinder the students' progress!"

The oblivious students eyed Cayna doubtfully, unsure of whether she would be able to manage okay.

The knights, however, knew their captain's "girlfriend" was no ordinary person. The other adventurers recognized her abilities as well, so no one was particularly concerned. Rather, they had an unusual amount of faith and felt no need to panic unless she did. In truth, Cayna herself didn't realize this for a single second.

Furthermore, several students had witnessed the altercation between Cayna and the nobleman during the River Festival and told their friends all about the adventurer who also happened to be the mother of their headmistress. Thanks to this, everyone and *their* mother were aware of her status before they'd even reached the halfway point... Like how she was the mother of both the High Priest and the Academy's headmistress, and that she was a skilled adventurer whose talents were even recognized by the royal family...

This was an undeniable fact, but Cayna also considered it an utter nuisance.

"Ah!" she cried. "I can feel Opus whining about me from afar!"

"What's gotten into you all of a sudden...?" Lonti asked.

Cayna poked fun at Opus to gloss over the sudden chill she felt. Shivering, she checked their surroundings with her Intuition skill and Kee's surveillance capabilities.

The Wind Spirits were in good condition and sensed no abnormalities. She'd instructed them to return if they discovered anything odd outside of battle and patrol, so Cayna wondered if this chill was only her imagination.

"What's the matter, Cayna?"

"Oh, it's nothing. I got a bad feeling, but there doesn't seem to be anything weird in the area..."

"Are you coming down with something?"

Lonti and Myleene looked concerned, but Cayna waved them off cheerfully. She decided Opus must be up to no good somewhere and mentally saved several jabs for later. Far away, Opus felt a similar chill. However, that had nothing to do with the story at hand.

"Oh, Cayna. Allow me to introduce you."

As they walked and chatted, Myleene introduced the three Imperial Knights.

"I pestered my mother to let me bring some of our most elite knights. This dragoid is..."

"I'm Helau. It's nice to meet you."

"A pleasure, milady. I am Sfult."

"Oh, uh, I'm Ark. Nice to meet you."

The gray dragoid Helau carried a huge two-handed sword on her back and quietly bowed to Cayna as if the blade were light as a feather.

Sfult was a brown-haired, blue-eyed elf. She lifted the hem of her skirt and offered a ladylike curtsy. Elves seemed to know that Cayna was a high elf, as this was the most reverent gesture one could give.

The knight named Ark was a black-haired, dark-eyed human who seemed to stumble over her words. She hurriedly pressed one hand to her chest and bowed to Cayna.

"If you're all elites, are you fine with being called out here? Don't you usually prioritize people in the castle?"

"Yes, well, that's normally the case. After all, we've never fought in a true war ever since the three nations were founded," replied Sfult.

"Actually," said Lonti, "Mye asked for volunteers throughout the castle, and ten times more than this showed up…"

"Wow…," Cayna marveled. She was tempted to mutter *And the Imperial Knights just went along with it?* but she held her tongue.

"In short, outside of training, everyone is twiddling their thumbs."

This final dam was spectacularly broken by the princess herself. Unable to contain themselves any longer, Lonti and Cayna burst into laughter and infected any student who heard. However, perhaps fearing their laughter would be taken as disrespect, many tried to hold it in. Instead, their shoulders trembled as they giggled in silence. Only a chorus of hollow laughter rose from the three Imperial Knights.

Once the students had calmed down, Helau raised a hand. "May I have a moment?"

"Sure, what's up?"

"Lady Cayna, you are Lady Mai-Mai's mother, correct?"

"Yep. And Skargo and Kartatz are my sons."

Cayna didn't really get it, but Helau and Sfult appeared satisfied by this answer. Ark, on the other hand, looked completely nonplussed and blinked in surprise.

"Pardon me, but do you happen to know anyone named Barzelan or Tolfossa?" asked Helau.

"Barzelan and…Tolhossa?"

"It's Tolfossa. I suppose you haven't met them, then," Sfult replied.

Mumbling to herself, Cayna crossed her arms and pretended think it over while she checked to see if either name was in Kee's log. The results were immediate but unfavorable.

"Hmm. Sorry, I haven't seen or heard of them."

"…I see. Thank you," said Helau.

She and Sfult were visibly disappointed. Myleene and Lonti, who were totally lost in the conversation, merely stood there flustered.

"Um, might I ask what is going on?"

"Have you three met?"

"Nope, not before today. But I'm pretty sure I know what you're trying to ask." Cayna recalled her Search on them earlier, then said something only a player would understand. "Helau, Sfult—you're both Foster Children, right?"

""What?!""

"Those names just now belong to players who might be your parents or siblings or whatever."

""Whaaaaaat?!""

"And you, Ark, are a player."

"Huh?"

Stupefied, Helau's and Sfult's mouths formed perfect circles. Ark, who had assumed she was safe outside the mosquito net, froze in shock like a deer in headlights.

Lonti and Myleene read the room and fell silent.

Cayna's bold assertion came from her Search of the three Imperial Knights—Helau was level 180, while Sfult was level 190. Ark went as high as level 230. All three were powerful in their own right and easily identifiable as either players or Foster Children.

However, Cayna could tell that Ark was a player since Search indicated a national affiliation in addition to her name and level. Helau and Sfult didn't have specific nationalities, so she determined they must be Foster Children. More importantly, Cayna dug deeper into a questionable point of Ark's player profile.

"Uh, Ark?"

"Y-yes! What is it?"

Trembling from head to toe, Ark straightened her posture. She was restless and looked more like a clumsy civil servant than a knight.

"So your display name is a reference to the Ark of the Covenant. Ark's an easy nickname to remember. I guess your *real* name is actually something like Ark of Darkness or Jet Black Ark, right?"

Ark gulped at Cayna's question, and after a good three seconds, the color drained from her face.

"N-nooooooooooooooo! Sh-sh-sh-sh-she can see my-my-my-my-my-my statssssssss!!"

She clearly hadn't been expecting this and started to yell and writhe in horror. Ark then crouched behind Helau and covered her eyes and ears. Everyone else was still on the move, so only Ark would be left behind. When she realized this and scurried to catch up like a little animal, all eyes were on her.

Ark's colleagues eyed her with pity. Each pressed a finger to their lips and whispered to the dot-eyed Myleene and Lonti, "Let's keep this between us."

"Who'd have thought I'd meet one of us here? I guess you really do have to go abroad to hear news of home. It's nice to meet you, Ark."

Once Cayna made it clear she understood the situation, Ark formulated a hypothesis.

"That means you're a player, too, Cayna? Wait... What? Then could Lady Mai-Mai and Sir Skargo be...? Huh?!"

"Yep. They're my foster kids."

Ark's eyes darted around as her expression went from *doubt* to *acceptance* to *doubt* again and then finally to *surprise* in quick succession.

"Little Ark is adorable as always," Helau and Sfult giggled as they watched her. Ark was apparently the mascot of their friend group.

"Seriously, are the Imperial Knights okay...?" Cayna wondered aloud.

"Well, these three usually escort us royals and patrol the castle, so they don't venture outside like this very often. I don't exactly understand what's going on, but I'm glad to see you've been enjoying yourself as well."

"Hmm. I'm glad they're not hounding me anyways. Sorry to keep so many secrets from you, Mye."

"I will lend an ear when you're ready to talk." Myleene beamed.

Cayna guiltily wondered how she'd even begin to explain the players.

"Perhaps you could say the world is a game board?"

That makes it sound like I'm calling everyone a chess piece or something. The reaction would be terrifying.

Explanation and persuasion weren't her forte, so Cayna thought maybe Opus should write the script instead.

"By the way," she began, "aren't you going to ride in your fancy royals-only carriage and flex in front of the other students?"

"Why would you even suggest something so shameless?!" cried Lonti.

"Am I wrong? I thought being condescending, abusing authority, and walking around like a big shot was part of the royal package."

"Cayna, I'm begging you. Please do not to apply such a strange value system to Mye or the rest of the royal family."

Lonti's expression was vaguely threatening, so Cayna continued nodding impulsively. "Royals aren't like that in this world, huh?"

"Most certainly not! They govern with honesty and integrity!"

"Okay, okay," Cayna replied, already done with the conversation.

She had turned away from Lonti when Ark trotted over to her and whispered, "Cayna, did you do a lot of quests for royals and nobles back in the game?"

"Ugh, sure did. I wanted to strangle and blow 'em up."

Cayna thought back to the NPC nobles and royalty in the Game Era. They were rude and arrogant, regarded anyone beneath their social rank as less than, and treated the working class like tools. They were also exceedingly cruel and did not hesitate to execute whoever invoked their ire.

Naturally, the players detested them like nothing else. NPCs weren't so easily avoided, and making the wrong choice in your interactions with them could land you in hot water, so there was really no option but to reluctantly accept every request. There were honest nobles as well, but these were only about one in twenty quests. After everything the Skill Masters had been through to claim their title, these nobility quests really tested the limits of their patience. It made their blood boil.

"I did one of those quests and hated it," said Ark.

"Right? Been there, done that," Cayna replied.

The two became fast friends as they secretly shared their *Leadale* experiences, and each new bit of common ground was followed by an inquiry on how the other got into it. Cayna had the Wind Spirits remain on lookout while she and Ark fell deeper into conversation. Both girls were still on guard duty and obviously couldn't forget their surroundings. However, Cayna was free to relegate everything to Kee, since he was completely automatic.

Based on the pair's discussion, Myleene assumed Ark and Cayna hailed from the same place—although since one was a human and the other a high elf, Myleene doubted their sole connection was a single homogeneous hometown. Thanks to knowledge passed down through the royal family, she had some understanding of the word *players*, which peppered their conversation.

She knew of the havoc they wreaked across the continent over two centuries earlier. Nevertheless, there were also tales of their impact on Leadale's geography, so she couldn't bring herself to label these "players" as all bad. As far as Myleene knew, Cayna and Shining Saber were people of moral character who never once ravaged the land in the fires of war (at least by modern opinion). Cayna's earlier reaction suggested she'd be open to questions if asked, so Myleene decided to patiently bide her time.

"Hee-hee-hee."

"Whatever is the—? Um, what's the matter, Mye?"

Lonti almost fell back into formal speech but hastily switched to the more casual tone of a close friend when Mye eyed her reproachfully.

"I'm sorry."

"You're still too stiff."

"This is the best I can do. I'm afraid I'm not like Cayna."

As far as Lonti and Mye were concerned, a high elf like Cayna was a dignified royal. It just didn't always look that way since she didn't boast this fact and sometimes even forgot it herself. She was also evidently all-powerful, which truly put Cayna in a league all her own.

"I'm saying it's hard to find someone who doesn't care about my social standing."

"It's hard to believe Cayna is a royal at all."

"Yes, that's certainly true," Myleene agreed with a laugh.

Lonti thought she'd deny it and felt a bit deflated.

"I wonder if I can pull that off, too?" Myleene said.

"Perhaps you ought to build up your strength first?"

"You're right. Considering how often Cayna causes a commotion, you would need to be quite strong just to survive."

Having realized such a goal was nigh impossible, the girls exchanged glances and laughed. Cayna continued chatting with Ark, unaware of Myleene and Lonti's conversation.

Helau and Sfult meant to remind Cayna of her guard duty, but since several visible Wind Spirits provided Cayna with detailed reports of their surroundings every few minutes, neither could do much more than bitterly acquiesce.

"I see," said Cayna. "So your little brother introduced you to

Leadale. You must like to stop and smell the roses if it took you a whole year to reach level 200."

"I did lots of offline quests or quests in town, plus I didn't fight very often," replied Ark. "Sometimes my brother's friends would help out and go hunting with me."

Cayna nodded along as she listened. The way Ark described her brother's friends seemed kind of...familiar?

The two continued to talk like old pals. Meanwhile, Helau and Sfult followed with the wagon.

"So you're not really suited to combat?" Cayna asked Ark. "I'm a little worried, since the area up ahead is pretty dangerous. You might have to make a run for it ASAP."

"I'm not totally useless in battle. I'll give it my best shot. This is my job, after all. I mainly use a bow, but I can act as indirect backup, too."

"Gwah?!"

Ark smiled uncomfortably as she unsheathed the weapon at her side. When Cayna used Search on it, she did a spit take and stared in amazement.

"Isn't that Impaler, the Ultimate Crossbow?! Where'd you get a super-rare weapon like this...?"

"This is just what I got when I made a crossbow."

The blade of the delicate ceremonial-looking sword split in half to create the gun barrel (the bow portion). Then, a grip and trigger appeared from the hilt and transformed into a crossbow. It was a beautiful projectile weapon accented in gold and silver. Its strength depended on the overall level of its wielder, but in addition to an auto-loading function that cost only a single MP, it was a Cheat weapon capable of rapid-fire.

The chances of producing a high-quality crossbow were one in a thousand, but an item of this caliber was more like one in a hundred million. Back in the game, it was a manufactured rare item that sold at auction for a record-breaking 700 million gil. In fact, as far as Cayna could remember, the weapon caused a stir at auction only twice in the three-plus years she'd been playing *Leadale*. People claimed that even a Skill Master couldn't replicate it.

"What dang luck…"

"No, I'm pretty sure my luck has already run out. My name is just one example."

"Come to think of it, why *does* it sound like it's got some shady history?"

"In those final hours of the game, I fell for a trap…"

"Huh?"

Ark explained in detail that she'd been dungeon-crawling and had gotten caught in a forced name-change trap. This was one of several possibilities with Active Skill: Trap Creation. After registering several random words, the prankster responsible could change the names of hapless players. These ranged from embarrassing to down-right cringey, and the only fix was to briefly log out, pay a fee, and edit your character settings. It was truly malicious.

Unfortunately, Ark got caught on *Leadale*'s final day and fell into this world without a chance to amend things. A classic case of bad timing.

"Ahhh, so *that's* why you shortened it to Ark."

"Oh, it's always been Ark. I didn't make any changes there. Actually, my little brother came up with the name. He was basically a *Leadale* junkie, plus he was a top-level player. Incredible, right?" Ark giggled.

A bead of sweat dripped down Cayna's forehead. It was tough to admit she was an addict, too, but there was no need to hide it, either. She mustered up the courage to ask the question on her mind.

"Um, we might've met if he was a top player… What was his name?"

"Erm, uh, let's see… Oh! It was something tasty sounding, like Tartar Sauce!"

"Tartar…Sauce? …Ah!"

Cayna knew the name all too well.

What a small world; the siblings' interdimensional travel was pretty incredible in its own way.

"Do you know him?" Ark asked.

"I do. His real name is Tartarus, though."

"Oh, yes, that's right. I knew it was Tarta-something."

Cayna felt bad for the guy; even his big sis was calling him Tartar Sauce.

"We were in the same guild, for better or worse. He and I are well acquainted."

"Huh? What? Cayna, you were in the Cream Cheese guild, too?! Does that mean you're a junkie like him?"

"'Junkie' is a bit… I mean, you're technically not wrong. Still, I'd rather you not call me that."

"Oh, I'm sorry. I'll stick to just Cayna."

No matter how accurate the label was, being called a junkie on a regular basis would get old quick. Cayna pressed a hand to her chest in relief when it didn't immediately stick.

"Huh," said Ark. "That explains things."

"What things?"

"I just felt like your name was somehow familiar. My brother must have mentioned you on occasion. Now I get it."

"…Mind giving an example of what he said about me?" Cayna asked, a vein in her temple visibly throbbing from anger.

It was unclear whether Ark took notice. She thought for a moment and then answered matter-of-factly:

"Something like how you're an emotional ticking time bomb and your obsession with magic is a danger to others. I always thought you sounded pretty scary, but now that we've met, I can see how wrong he was."

I knew it.

This answer didn't surprise Cayna in the least, although hearing it point-blank still struck a nerve. The target of her wrath was Tartarus/Exis, of course.

"Actually, I did run into your little brother here."

"What?! He came here, too?!"

"Huh?

"…Uhhh?"

Ark's blank-eyed stare confirmed that neither sibling had any clue the other had come to this world. Cayna spoke with Exis on multiple occasions, but the topic of siblings never came up. She didn't recall him mentioning any, either.

"Can I see him?" Ark asked.

"Yeah, sure. This is good timing, so let me contact him."

"Really?! Thank you very much, Cayna!"

Seeing Ark's face light up made Cayna feel warm and fuzzy inside. She considered dropping vague hints about Ark to tease Exis, but that seemed wrong.

So she opened the Friend Message screen and wrote to him: Just ran into ur sister lol.

As thanks for the unflattering rumors Exis had spread about her to Ark, Cayna blocked any incoming messages from him. She grinned mischievously and wondered how he would manage to come find her. An ominous, arabesque cloud effect rumbled above her; she let slip a chilling cackle, and everyone in the general vicinity slowly backed away.

Meanwhile, Exis and Quolkeh were in the remote village under the pretext of a vacation. They had initially planned to enjoy the tourney and took the outer eastern trade route from Helshper to Felskeilo, but...

Their first impression at the village entrance was *Damn, that chick has some nerve!*

The village wasn't particularly big, but it was surrounded by a solid wall with gargoyle sentries situated at intervals atop the perimeter. There was also a bathhouse that looked to be made of cypress wood with separate areas for men and women. And to top it all off, a giant projector sat in a corner of the tavern.

"The hell is Cayna doin' to this place?!" Exis raged, the memories from last time still fresh in his mind.

It wasn't long before Roxilius noticed Exis and Quolkeh's arrival and took them to see Luka. Later, the two turned to jelly as they slowly savored the wonders of the bathhouse.

Quite some time later, both adventurers still had yet to leave the village.

There was delicious food at the inn, and they could check on Felskeilo from the projector. The cost of living was also much cheaper than in the capital. Sakaiya's village branch carried a large selection of products, and a mermaid would do their laundry for a reasonable price. The little hamlet lacked for nothing. Soon, the two adventurers started making themselves comfortable.

"Maybe I'll retire here once my adventuring days are over," Exis announced.

"Sign me up."

Steam gently rose from Exis's and Quolkeh's armor as they collapsed on to one of the tavern tables. Neither resembled a seasoned adventurer in the least.

Moreover, no one criticized them or complained. It made sense that these two were as laid-back as Gude**** right now.

"Hrm..."

Nonetheless, there was one tiny objection. It came from Luka, the girl they had personally rescued.

""Hey, Luka.""

She sulked moodily and glared at Exis and Quolkeh, who were still collapsed on the table.

"What's wrong?" asked Quolkeh. "You'll waste that cute little face scowling like that."

"When your greatest heroes are slumped over like fools in public, how can one not be disheartened?" came a voice—it was Roxine, who stood attentively by Luka's side.

"Gweh?!"

Her contemptuous glare sent a chill down Exis's spine as if he'd been struck by a glacier. He hastily sat up.

Thinking back on it, he recognized that shameless attitude that hurled abuse at her own master. When Exis first met this paid-content NPC back in his guild, her rapid-fire insults had filled him with terror.

"Heh-heh-heh. Look at how comfortable you are—beheading you would be such a simple task," Roxine whispered, already right next to Quolkeh and stroking her neck.

"Eek?!"

Quolkeh paled. Any warm and fuzzy feelings from earlier were long gone now that this hostility had enveloped their corner of the tavern. Luka, meanwhile, had no idea what was going on.

"You... Are you here to warn us on Cayna's orders?" Exis asked Roxine, reaching out a hand to help Quolkeh. Roxine swiftly dodged him and slipped into his blind spot.

"Unfortunately, we are forbidden from killing anyone in this village except for those who pose a threat. Thank your lucky stars, you failure of a dragon."

It was the worst insult you could give a dragoid, and Exis

instinctively bristled. It didn't cut him too deep since he was a player, but he understood the nuance, thanks to his fellow dragoids.

"You tryin' to start something with us?"

As soon as Exis threatened Roxine, she returned to her position behind Luka to preserve the tavern's jovial atmosphere.

"Sadly, I can only offer you candid advice in Lady Luka's stead. Please do not utter such vile language in front of her," Roxine said, as if nothing had happened.

Quolkeh stood. "What the heck?! Speak for yourself— Exis?!"

"I don't think she's acting on Cayna's orders," Exis muttered cautiously, trying to placate his partner.

Lytt had been milling around the tavern, and Luka ran to her when her friend called her over. Now that there were no innocent bystanders, Exis had some newfound confidence.

"Keh-keh-keh-keh." Roxine chuckled quietly.

"What's so funny?"

I can take her down now without looking bad in front of Luka, he thought. However, he kept his mouth shut and watched Roxine's every move.

"Can your addled brain not even comprehend your own authority?"

"What?"

"Take a good look at yourselves, you numbskulls."

What's she after?

After a bit of trolling on her part, Roxine left to join Luka. Exis slumped back into his chair, miffed over this lost opportunity to trade blows.

Luine came over with snacks and alcohol and placed them on the table.

"Bee in your bonnet, fellas?" she asked. "Weren't you just in the baths?"

The fear in Quolkeh's eyes made her freeze. Exis looked completely wiped out. Neither seemed the least bit refreshed. Luine had already seen them around for several days and could tell something was off. She cocked her head curiously.

"...What *was* that...?" Exis wondered aloud.

Once Luine left, a strange silence hovered over them. Quolkeh massaged her stiff facial muscles.

"I thought I was gonna die...," she muttered.

"That's the stain of Cream Cheese," said Exis. "She's an infamously malicious maid..."

"The hell are you talking about?"

"She turned out that way back when the NPCs came to life, and we just experienced it firsthand...," he replied stiffly.

Exis reached for the snacks and explained what they'd just witnessed. This was something only his fellow guild members would immediately pick up on, and now Quolkeh did, too.

"She said something about authority—what does that even mean?" Quolkeh asked, nervously fiddling with her tankard.

Exis racked his brain for a moment but finally struck a fist against his palm. "If she was talkin' about player authority, it must be our stats or skills, right?"

"Oh, so *that's* it..."

Quolkeh nodded and checked her status screen, but nothing seemed off. Exis took a peek at his own.

Quolkeh was about to ask what his screen looked like, but the words caught in her throat when she saw his shocked expression.

"Wh-what's wrong?" she said.

"......"

"H-huh? Heyyy, Exiiiis?"

That shock turned to fear. Quolkeh got ready to slap him across the face when he didn't respond. However, just as she swung her arm back, Exis suddenly stood. His expression was ghastly.

"…We're leaving," he said out of the blue.

"…Huh?" said Quolkeh, absolutely clueless as to what was going on.

"I can't take this!"

Exis promptly beat a retreat and dashed up the stairs.

Quolkeh stayed put, utterly bewildered.

CHAPTER 3
Camping, a Barrier, an Advance, and Preparations

The students and faculty continued their journey and arrived at the campground before orange even tinged the sky.

In the middle of the forest, there was a clearing that stretched about one hundred meters in diameter. Nonetheless, the area's limited use had attracted overgrown weeds that rose high above their heads. Deeper within, some even began to resemble full-grown trees.

First, Cayna and the other adventurers made sure the coast was clear.

"Get lost."

At her imperious command, the weeds scurried away like small frightened animals and relocated to elsewhere in the forest. Adventurers and students alike witnessed the wondrous phenomenon with mouths agape.

"Leave it to the high elves to control nature. That was nuts."

"I wasn't too sure if I could pull it off," said Cayna. "I'm surprised this worked out, to be honest."

"Thanks. I feel *real* safe now!" Cohral replied sarcastically while everyone else stood frozen in front of them.

Once the Swift Horses had regained their composure and confirmed the area was secure, the students rushed in. Apparently, someone in the past had run on ahead and diffused an aroma to attract the monsters, so a minimum amount of precaution was necessary.

"Why spark terror like that...?"

"I don't know the full details, but the weeds release a noxious smell when uprooted. Thanks to that, the monsters came runnin'. It was pretty rough."

"You witnessed it? Thank you for your service."

"The monsters weren't too bad, but that stench alone was a *nightmare*."

"Even our clothes reeked!"

Laughter rose from the Swift Horses as they conversed. Dealing with the stench sounded far worse than fighting the monsters. As for the terrorist responsible for this noxious mess—after ducking into the forest to watch their victims suffer, they were severely injured by a horned bear that attacked from behind. It was a pretty foul story.

The students used this past tragedy to better arm themselves. However, Cayna listened closely to the trees around her and confirmed no monster threats lurked nearby.

"Being a high elf must be so convenient."

"There are pros and cons," said Cayna. "I can also hear the screams of the forest straight into my brain."

"Ack."

The students set to work while Cayna spoke with the Swift Horses. Once the instructors divided everyone into three teams and assigned each a specific role, they set to work.

One group began pitching the tents that would serve as their sleeping quarters; another left with Cohral, the Armor of Victory, and the teachers to procure water from a nearby stream. The remaining group went to gather firewood in the forest with the Swift Horses.

"Hey, can't we sift through whatever those clumps of weeds left behind and burn that instead?"

"Ms. Cayna, we can't just use raw wood right away."

"No problem. I can evaporate the water in an instant."

"That won't do us students any good! Please don't bother!"

The teachers and some of the students had placed a spell barrier around the campsite. Unsurprisingly, Myleene and Lonti remained inside the camp. Since Mai-Mai saw Cayna as their last line of defense, she inevitably stayed back as well.

The three Imperial Knights took the luggage from the wagon and opened it flat on the ground. It started expanding into a large two-room tent that stretched five meters in every direction, and several metal poles built the framework. It was complete within twenty minutes. Cayna peeked inside curiously.

"Ohhh, nice," she said. "I feel like I've seen this somewhere before..."

"The concept isn't so different from our old world," said Ark.

Thoroughly impressed, Cayna brought up examples she'd seen online while Ark produced tables and such from her Item Box. The three Imperial Knights had apparently divided the interior furniture between themselves and brought it along in their Item Boxes. One room was a dining space, and the other was for sleeping. Only players and Foster Children could transport furniture in this extraordinary way.

"Sakaiya carries similar items, though, so they aren't too difficult to obtain."

"Oh, this one is pretty common. I thought it was a special nobles-only item."

"I heard a player who loved camping first proposed it."

"Huh. Maybe I should ask Caerick."

They prepared quickly, and Lonti had brewed tea by the time Myleene entered the tent.

Cayna was invited to join them, but she declined since she was supposed to be on guard duty. Ark and the other two Imperial Knights alternated in shifts, with one person inside and two outside, so Cayna's responsibilities were elsewhere.

"Well then, what to do?"

While Helau and Sfult kept a close eye on the area, Cayna had Wind Spirits silence the weeds' screams. The voices of the weeds were distinct from those of the trees, and she could clearly sense their sorrow. Still, that didn't mean she enjoyed listening to it. One can't silence feelings with a simple breeze, however, and the gossip-loving Wind Spirits who prattled on excitedly were only a temporary consolation.

The three Wind Spirits Cayna had summoned at the start of their journey were all level 110. Each was a semitransparent green and looked like a beautiful little girl who stood about four heads tall. As the spirits twittered and danced around Cayna, they would sometimes use her hair or sleeves to play tag or hide-and-seek.

It was clear they were following the students' example, but evidently the summoned spirits weren't supposed to be quite so visible. Moreover, anyone unlearned in magic shouldn't have been able to hear their whispers, let alone catch their appearance.

Invisibility was out of the question back in the game, so Cayna and Cohral hadn't taken much notice. She tried to come up with an excuse, but students and faculty alike had already deemed her an eccentric who employs powerful spirits. Silence alone had already put wild ideas in everyone's heads, so Cayna did nothing more than stare off into the far distance.

The group who had gone to fetch water soon returned and began their dinner preparations. The students' tents were shaped like toppled triangle prisms and large enough to accommodate four or five people. White-and-brown-spotted animal hides covered a framework supported by slender yet firm lumber.

In the meantime, preparation and surveillance of the area was handled exclusively by the students. Although Ark and her fellow Imperial Knights had been assigned to protect the princess, the entire purpose of this event was to help the students gain experience. The camp supervisor and older men even told Cayna to keep the Wind Spirits' assistance within moderation.

Since not everyone could use such convenient methods, logic dictated it wouldn't benefit the students to rely on them. This wasn't Cohral's first survival event, and he told Cayna the adventurers wouldn't have much to do except kill time or maybe teach, unless there was an emergency. She decided to play it by ear.

"I'll admit my idea of camping *is* pretty heavy-handed," Cayna said. She scrolled through her memories as she watched small bonfires light up near each tent for dinner.

Every camp outing so far had been summons-centric:

A Fire Spirit to make a woodless campfire and keep the flames burning.

A White Dragon to use as a naturally fluffy bed and blanket.

A Brown Dragon to keep watch, since she couldn't use a Charm Barrier.

Cohral noticed Cayna standing around with a blank stare and grew suspicious.

"Hey, Cayna. Don't you have a tent or something?" he called. "Or are you gonna stay with the princess?"

"Absolutely not. What kind of guard would I be if I slept the night away?"

"You'll crash and burn if you go nonstop."

"Then I'll just cast Sleep Be Gone."

Even so, this skill wasn't ideal, since it promised to knock you out for several days afterward.

"You can't really join a bunch of gross dudes like us, but what about the Swift Horses in the girls' camp?"

"Nah. I'm a part of this group, too, so a pelt is enough."

"...A pelt?"

Cayna dispelled the Wind Spirits and startled nearby onlookers when she cast another white magic circle.

"Come, White Divine Beast!"

"Wait, wait, wait, wait! What do you think you're summoning?!" Cohral shouted as he tried in vain to stop her impromptu decision. White light poured from a summons circle, and an enormous snowy mass appeared before Cayna.

It had a fluffy coat you could definitely bury your head into. All present—with a few exceptions—stared in wide-eyed shock. Their jaws practically touched the ground.

The creature appeared to be a weasel. It was six meters tall and covered in pure white fur. Despite a commanding size, it looked much like any normal weasel. The biggest difference was the second pair of eyes above its normal ones.

"*Kyuuu,*" it squeaked adorably.

The white beast bowed to its master Cayna, then stood on its hind legs. Its whiskers twitched as it surveyed the area restlessly. All the while, the weasel didn't forget to wrap the thick, luxurious tail that took up a third of its body around her.

One breathless, petrified bystander after another shriveled up and fell to the ground under its sharp four-eyed leer.

Myleene peeked her head from the tent to investigate the commotion and stared at the white weasel incredulously.

Cohral, unlike the rest who cowered before the snowy creature, lambasted Cayna.

"Yo, c'mon! Warn people before you summon somethin' like that outta nowhere! Look, everyone is scared stiff!"

"Okay?"

"Don't act like you don't know what I'm talking about! Anyway, what *is* that thing? I can't read its level, and I've never seen it before in my life!"

Cayna raised one hand to lightly beckon the creature, and the vigilant, four-eyed large weasel stooped to rub its head against her. Myleene and Lonti watched Cayna stroke its soft pelt and blushed as if remembering the touch of the White Dragon.

No longer bound by the summons's scowl, the students and everyone else observed from a cautious distance as Cayna introduced it to Cohral.

"This is the Great Weasel of Euphoria. It's a rare monster from the Hermit Area."

"That's shady as hell..."

Even Cayna had to smirk at the strange name as she said it. It sounded like some kind of quack cure-all a sketchy religion might tout.

The Euphoria part was a nickname among the players, but its official name was Hermit Beast Izunae. This monster was level 450 and, as the name implied, only found in the Hermit Area. It wasn't a *rare* monster, per se, but simply one that was difficult to defeat. Thanks to special abilities like Flee and Good Fortune, escape was the creature's specialty. It would run for the hills before players even had a chance to encounter it and would scurry off if anyone so much as looked at it from afar or happened to cross its path.

Guildmasters at the time agreed the Hermit Beast was completely pointless as an Active Monster. It was notoriously difficult to catch, and the flood of complaints made to the Admins reflected this. Izunae managed to elude even the fastest of guild members, which perpetuated rumors that it was a rare monster.

This activity pattern meant it was rare to encounter them in the Hermit Area, and fighting one was practically impossible. Cayna and the others had tried human wave tactics and magically carpet-bombing within several widespread barriers. After several attempts, they finally succeeded. It took a total of thirty-five people a full night in real time. This included thirteen Skill Masters, making the battle unprecedented in *Leadale* history.

If Izunae was appointed as a summons rather than eliminated, its unique abilities served both parties and summoners. Flee wasn't used often, but Good Fortune increased one's drop item rate and resistance against status ailments. It also improved the effectiveness of poison of an ally's special attack (such as poison or paralysis) and increased the chance of a critical hit, so it was useful both offensively and defensively. Izunae's physical attacks were limited to biting and scratching, which really only hampered Limit Breakers like Cayna in a typical hunt. Overall, it was considered an option that desperately clung to your party like a bad cold once summoned.

Cayna had called upon Izunae this time for its soft white fur. And like the previous White Dragon, she wanted it for one single purpose—to use as a living, breathing blanket.

Even so, a dragon summoned at the lowest level was still a dragon. Cayna wasn't sure how eyewitnesses would react to a creature regarded as myth and legend, but this time around everyone had unanimously stiffened when she summoned Izunae.

"Huh?"

"Who wouldn't be scared?! That thing you just summoned looks like it can swallow people whole!" Cohral shouted, accurately voicing the concerns of all present.

The students' tents were clustered at the center of the campsite and dotted with bonfires. The adventurers had their own arrangements, but the four Swift Horses and five Armor of Victory members positioned themselves on opposite sides of the central bonfire. Their basic strategy was to wrap up in blankets and take turns sleeping in a huddle. The students would spearhead the night watch, but the adventurers were there to provide guidance on how to pass the night and perceive outside threats. Cayna followed suit and positioned herself near Myleene and Lonti's tent along the camp's perimeter. This would allow Izunae's heightened senses to detect danger and give Cayna the greatest defensive advantage. Furthermore, even if Cayna failed to notice nearby hostiles, her Anti-Perv AutoGuard summons would pick up the slack. However, this was strictly for emergencies only.

Mai-Mai said Cayna could unleash her full might if the princess was in danger (Mai-Mai: "I certainly did not!"), so she had a solid excuse.

Cayna figured their biggest threat here was quest monsters prowling around the continent and shouldered the responsibility of bodyguard. She was the first to volunteer if anyone needed a job done.

Mai-Mai herself informed the rest of the faculty about this, so no questions were raised. Cayna had initially thought the whole escort gig was a pain but appreciated Cohral's help as a go-between.

As the students (including the princess) skillfully prepared dinner, the faculty and party leaders planned that night's patrol schedule.

"Um, can we talk for a sec?"

"Oh, Cayna. Is there something you'd like to add?"

Everyone turned to Cayna as she approached the group with a raised hand.

"I'm quite sure we mentioned that we'd be using a different system."

"You did, but I just wanted to check in, since I'll be gone for a few hours tonight."

"Ah, yes. The headmaster said you had business to attend to. We don't mind, but you did accept this escort position. Are you sure it's all right to leave?"

"It's only for the night, and Izunae will be here. I don't think it's a problem. I can call out another summons, depending on the situation."

Cohral grimaced at that last sentence. The creatures Cayna summoned were generally high-level and far outside this world's idea of common sense. Many looked like unknown monsters, and if any aspiring adventurers had a terrifying encounter with one outside the city, he feared it would lead to road closures.

"Hey."

"What's up, Cohral? You've got a scary look on your face."

"Don't summon anything too crazy. It'll cause all kinds of problems if people misunderstand and can't go outside," Cohral warned, pointing at Izunae. The weasel was curled up in a donut but exuding a commanding presence.

"But it's adorable," Cayna insisted.

"Yeah, maybe to *you*!"

She frowned in disappointment. Cohral had more experience with the general population, though, so she took heed and summoned a cat. It was the cath palug that had stayed back to protect

Luka during the River Festival in the capital. Cayna handed the pure white kitten to Myleene and Lonti, and they grinned from ear to ear.

"*Meooow.*"

""It's…it's…it's so cuuuute!""

"Cath palug, please watch over these two."

"*Meooow.*"

Although it was kitten-like at the moment, the cath palug's true form was akin to a fierce panther. It could change size at will and was far more powerful than Izunae, at level 600. As the cath palug's summoner, Cayna kept it a harmless-looking kitten, but it could nonetheless kill Cohral in an instant.

Given that Cayna had perhaps used Search on the cath palug, Cohral's face soured as he took a step back. He probably got a bad feeling.

Around the campsite, the students continued to prepare dinner. Although the adventurers had their own foodstuffs on hand, the Swift Horses were friendly with the students and decided to eat with them.

Cohral and his Armor of Victory boiled a jumbled mess of ingredients into a soup and ate it with tough salted bread. Meanwhile, Cayna paid the curious adventurers no mind as she casually processed the meat, vegetables, smoked fish, and water she brought with Cooking Skill: Witch's Brew. This versatile soup could be made with any three or more ingredients and restored 10 percent HP and MP. Since the standard recovery amount was one-tenth of the caster's HP and MP, Cayna's Witch's Brew was an unparalleled magical panacea.

As usual, it was finished in a literal flash and caught the attention of every student. For whatever reason, the end result resembled a pot of chopped ingredients floating in a bubbling purple liquid.

Onlookers instinctively took one step back from the mysterious mess. Those were the actual graphics back in the game, so Cayna broke into a sweat over what she'd concocted. Cohral winced.

"So, that's what Witch's Brew looks like in real life..."

"Um, I think I'll pass..."

"The students are watching. Eat it."

"...Right. I'll try to keep it down."

Sadness and resignation fell upon Cayna as Cohral, the only one who knew the truth of the situation, dealt a final blow. The Great Weasel of Happiness turned away from the purple steam and placed a paw on its master's shoulder.

Tears in her eyes, Cayna dipped a spoon into the purple liquid. The crowd nervously watched her take a bite.

"Tastes like hospital food," she concluded.

Cayna polished off the rest of the Witch's Brew, but concern spread among the students when one brave teacher who had agreed to try some fainted. It wasn't poisonous, though, so the teacher was simply moved to a tent. By the next day, it was like nothing had ever happened.

"Must be 'cause you made it, Cayna. Wasn't it packed with MP?" Cohral said.

As everyone took up their positions for night patrol, Cayna asked Izunae to search out nearby enemies and had the cath palug guard Myleene and the others.

"Please be careful, Cayna."

"You got it. I'll be back by tomorrow morning at the latest."

The Abandoned Capital barrier wasn't too far. Including the time it would take to check out the situation, Cayna expected three hours total. Unless something popped up along the way, she figured matters would be more or less settled by sunrise.

"I'm not too worried, since it's you, but this world can be unpredictable," Cohral warned Cayna. "Don't let your guard down."

"Right, thanks. I'm counting on you, too, Supreme Swordsman."

"You got it. And don't call me that."

"Ha-ha-ha. Well, I'm off."

With a wave of her cloak, Cayna headed into the dark forest as a sea of eyes watched anxiously. A number of students thought she was nuts and had a death wish.

When Cayna's figure receded, Izunae uncurled itself and stood on its hind legs to survey the area. Several students stiffened, but Cohral called out to them.

"Don't panic! That creature is just keeping an eye out for enemies. It means us no harm!"

As Cohral said, Izunae's ears and nose were concentrated on the surrounding vicinity. It did nothing more than twitch its whiskers repeatedly. Several people gave a deep sigh of relief, but the Armor of Victory's leader, a male mage, rebuked Cohral.

"You'll attract every monster around if you yell like that," he said.

"Oops. Sorry." Cohral scratched his head in apology, and his party members burst into laughter.

"Hey, if that happens, we'll just have the great Supreme Swordsman cut 'em down."

"Quit it! What am I supposed to do if you praise me like that and people realize I'm just an average swordsman?"

"Then we'll beg them for forgiveness."

"You make it sound like it's my fault!"

The students watched the Armor of Victory's comedy routine and envied their fearlessness of the night. The Swift Horses had intended to ease their nerves with humor as well. Jild's shoulders slumped when he realized he'd been beaten to the punch.

* * *

"Enemy sighted."

"Seriously?!"

Meanwhile, Cayna made a beeline through the forest to the barrier but screeched to a halt when Kee suddenly detected an enemy. She was still only a few hundred meters from the campsite.

"Ahead of me?"

"Correct. There are many."

"Tch! It's like they knew I was going to the Abandoned Capital!"

Cayna immediately summoned Cerberus.

"Cerberwoof! Sneak around from behind so we can pincer 'em!"

"""*Woof!*"""

The three-headed wolf-dog that came out of the magic circle crouched low to the ground and then raced off into the woods on the right. When her internal radar indicated an incoming cluster of glowing red dots, Cayna whipped out Hungry Like the Wolf from her Item Box and wielded a Rune Blade as well.

"Geh-geh-geh-geh-geh!"

The thicket ahead rustled and cracked as a group of armored goblins peeked their heads out.

"The Favelle Regional Guard?!"

The goblin fighters wore leather armor, and over half wielded stone axes and spears. The rest were goblin archers and mages equipped with bows and wands.

"Hold up. Aren't there, like, sixty here?!"

"Perhaps they account for more than one quest?"

A look of impatience shot across Cayna's face at the huge discrepancy between the quest monsters she'd expected and the quest monsters she got.

The Favelle Regional Guard was originally a group of twelve quest monsters. This was five times that. Each was also level 200, which made them a collective powerhouse. A level-400-ish player could normally take on the quest with a party without issue. Although Kee's defensive shield currently repelled their attack, the rain of arrows and magic missiles was a chilling scene.

"Gigiii!"

"Wha?!"

In addition, rather than closing in on their quarry, the presumed goblin leader in the back gave the command to spread out. One unit advanced toward Cayna, but the rest went off in twos and threes in every direction.

Cayna was powerful but alone, so this battle was to their advantage. After all, although she couldn't let them go a step farther, the enemy had the option to avoid conflict.

"There seem to be a few intelligent monsters in the mix."

"This is no time to be impressed! Kuu, help me out!"

Cayna cast a spell as she sought the hidden fairy's aid.

Magic Skill: Spatial Stagnation Zari Rael: Ready Set

"Take this!"

A blueish white electric net fifteen meters in diameter covered the goblins who charged straight at her. Sparks flew everywhere as they were entangled in a web of pain and paralysis. The monsters were reduced to charcoal in an instant. Cayna didn't even wait long enough to witness their demise before swinging the Rune Blade in her left hand and slicing in half the goblin mages who tried to flee.

Answering Cayna's plea, Kuu popped out into the air. After assessing the situation with a vicious glare, she sent a hail of red arrows down on a few goblins who had tried to escape to the right.

No, it was more than a hail; the arrows were like a violent torrent that tore the three to pieces.

"Yay me!"

"A bit overkill, though."

Kuu's innocent joy was terrifying.

One group led by the goblin commander was quickly slain by the Cerberus's ferocious claws and fangs when it sneaked up on them from behind.

When Cayna checked her internal radar, the scattered goblins had split into two main groups, with one heading northeast and the other south. Since there were fewer enemies to the south, she left those to the Cerberus and chased the goblins escaping to the northeast. She continued straight ahead and eventually reached the main road leading to Felskeilo's western gate. She kept a close eye on her radar, but at a certain point, the goblins suddenly disappeared off the map.

"What?"

Confused, Cayna came to an abrupt halt just as a cross-shaped flash shot at her from the opposite side of the road. There was no question it was some kind of blade technique, but she realized a head-on collision was imminent and instantly cast Air Blast Blade Giga Gohron, which she'd added to her shortcut list. The powerful wind jet and cross-flash clashed, and both attacks vanished into thin air. At the same time, a massive blade swung down from the forest. Cayna crossed the Rune Blade and Hungry Like the Wolf together to absorb it.

"Cayna?!"

"Exis?!"

Her attacker was someone Cayna knew all too well. The puzzled Exis held his strike position for a moment but jumped out of the way when he noticed a large shadow pass over Cayna to swoop down on him.

"""Raaaaagh!"""

"A Cerberus?!"

"Cerberwoof! Down, boy! He's not an enemy!"

After chomping the goblins to death as Cayna asked, Cerberus had followed from behind and quickly determined the figure crossing swords with its master must be trouble. The beast was about to leap into action again when Cayna called a time-out. Fangs still bared, it now growled by her side.

To prove he bore no ill will, Exis returned his massive blade to the sheath on his back. Quolkeh came up from behind with her whip in hand.

"Exis, I've taken care of things on my end," she said. "Whoa—Cayna?!"

"Oh, Quolkeh. You're here, too."

"Were those *your* goblins just now?"

While not exactly hostile, both eyed Cayna suspiciously. Since the goblins came from the same direction, they had mistakenly assumed she was the one who unleashed them.

"Nope, it wasn't me," Cayna told them. "Only demons can summon goblins."

"Then isn't there a chance Opus handled the summons and you brought 'em along?"

"Of course not! I was attacked, too, so stop jumping to weird conclusions!" she exclaimed, thoroughly tired of these odd misunderstandings.

"Fair enough," Exis said apologetically, seemingly convinced.

Quolkeh, meanwhile, wasn't following the conversation at all, so Cayna explained why she'd left the camp.

"I get your point," Quolkeh began, "but that's not what I wanna hear."

"Huh?" said Cayna.

Exis was unusually fidgety; he brought his threatening dragoid face close to Cayna's.

"Exis has been acting weird ever since he got this one message from you," Quolkeh went on. "He teleported us to Felskeilo in the middle of the night, threatened the guard and busted through the gate, then spotted a bunch of goblins and yelled, 'What is this, a test?!' and started going off the rails. Think of the poor soul who had to deal with all that crap."

She wearily took a canteen from her Item Box and started chugging it.

"Wow, good work," said Cayna.

"Ain't nothin' good about it!" griped Exis. "What the heck was that message earlier?"

"'Earlier'?"

"Don't act like you forgot. I mean the one you sent about my sister!"

"Ohhh!" Cayna pressed a palm to her fist upon remembering. "You mean Ark?"

"Hurry up and tell me where she is."

"Chill out, Exis," Quolkeh cut in, yanking him backward, "Cayna can't talk if you're in her face like that."

Exis was obviously worried about his sister. Cayna considered foisting her escort mission on him and decided to reveal Ark's location.

"Ark's on guard duty over there…"

As soon as Cayna specified his sister's place of work, Exis raced past her toward the camp. Cayna and Quolkeh watched in mute amazement.

"Um, I'll follow him," Quolkeh told Cayna.

"Uh, right. Good plan. He might be mistaken as a shady character and captured."

Izunae was one thing, but the cath palug would spring into action if it deemed him a serious threat. It boasted a strength no armor could match, and Exis would need backup if he didn't want to be taken out while wildly barreling toward the camp.

After Quolkeh disappeared into the night, Kuu finally returned to Cayna. They looked at each other, and Cayna sighed. She decided to return to her earlier route.

As Cayna approached the Abandoned Capital's barrier, she glanced around and frowned.

"This is pretty terrible…"

Most people wouldn't be able to see the semitransparent film barrier, but Cayna's Magic Eye and Magic Perception skills were at full throttle and highlighted the condition of the present barrier.

The curved surface, originally smooth as a pearl, had countless cracks running all throughout it. One section even had a giant hole in it. The barrier's restorative functions hung on by a thread, but even if the hole were filled, widespread cracks across other areas threatened to open in a domino effect. The barrier wasn't just nicked all over; it was clearly on the verge of collapse.

"This is all because Opus did a rush job," Cayna mumbled.

Suddenly, the barrier rippled next to her. Thinking this signaled that monsters were on their way, Cayna wasted no time and entered a battle stance. However, both a discreet figure and a sinister one appeared before her in tandem. Such a combination was rare, and Cayna's eyes went wide.

They were an angel and a demon. The first was a young female angel with four white wings. The other was a headless tree in the

shape of a person. The misplaced head was a white skull in a cavity on the right side of its chest.

Bristling with caution, Kuu prepared for battle. However, Cayna recognized the angel and demon.

"Wow, never thought I'd run into an argent and an Old Hollow here," she said with her usual candor.

Next to the relieved angel, the wooden demon pitched forward.

"O-Old Hollow?! I'll have you know that my kind are called shubez!"

"Uhhh, what were these guys called again, Kee?" Cayna mumbled with a puzzled head tilt.

"That is the name I have on record."

Old Hollow was a popular nickname for this creature among the players. It was short for Old Man Hollow, so named for the demon's distinct appearance. It was categorized as a demon and also referred to shubez monsters commonly found in the Underworld. Usually between level 400 and 500 on average, these weren't much of a threat compared to the rest of the area. However, they *could* meld with a level-800 monster. Once this happened, it would spam weakening spells and curses on players. No monster was more irritating.

The general rule in any party was to have a vanguard neutralize the main threat while the mages destroyed the shubez. Since the monster's body was a tree, most used a midlevel (for Cayna anyway) fire spell to burn it to a crisp.

An argent, on the other hand, was a monster from the Heaven Area who defended her sanctuary as its gatekeeper. She appeared as a female angel with four white wings and was an impressive level 700. Nonetheless, battle was not an argent's forte. Her only duty was to maintain a defensive wall around the sanctuary, so a host of divine followers fought on the front lines instead.

Back in the day, Cayna and several other Cream Cheese guild members shaved down an argent by breaking holes in the barrier while tackling the angelic horde. They would attack the argent before the holes were filled and eventually won after repeating this process a dozen or so times.

And now both were right before Cayna's eyes. They obviously weren't hostile, so she dropped her guard. A wary Kuu noticed this and swooped down to sit in her usual position.

"I take it you've got some kind of business with me, since you came all this way?" Cayna asked the two monsters.

The shubez and argent paused a few steps from Cayna and then fell to their knees with heads bowed.

"*We were summoned by Master Opuskettenshultheimer,*" said the shubez.

"You are his sworn friend," the argent added. "We shall not dare raise a blade to you, Lady Cayna."

"Ah, I knew it. Opus said I'd probably run into you...," Cayna muttered quietly with a smirk of realization.

"*Indeed.*"

"*Actually, Master Opus informed us of your arrival, Lady Cayna.*"

"That was totally unnecessary. He couldn't bother to fill me in?"

Cayna and Opus saw each other all the time. If he had something to say, she wished he'd just spit it out.

"*We've been keeping an eye on you, too.*"

"Come again?!"

When she asked for clarification, the answer was pretty straightforward.

The shubez had been observing Cayna's overall activities. Since the day she'd first arrived in Felskeilo, the monster had watched from a reasonable distance in the darkness and the shadows. In addition to reporting all this information to Opus, its mission was to prevent unexpected interference from third parties. When Cayna was targeted by organized crime, the Old Hollow pretended to be one of the Five Great Dukes for the sole purpose of eliminating them. In truth, it wasn't a shady character at all.

"So, that's why I randomly felt him nearby. I never signed off on this!"

Cayna puffed out her cheeks, but then she noticed the argent, who remained unfazed and wore a placid smile.

"Are you the one maintaining the Abandoned Capital's barrier?" she asked the angel.

"Indeed, I am."

Cayna had fought the argent countless times and understood her ecosystem (?), so she already comprehended the situation. The static noise around the angel was hard to miss—this monster couldn't hold her form much longer.

"I'm surprised Opus could keep this up for two hundred years."

"I do not understand it myself, but it seems I am rooted to this place."

"Right. I guess that's the special ability Opus mentioned."

"His connection will hold up as long as the target isn't destroyed."

Cayna could understand calling out a single summons like an argent, but there was also an entire army of low-level angels. An argent was better equipped to defend the main stronghold while the other angels eliminated any outside threats. Her Special Skill, Fence, was a unique and rare ability unavailable to players.

A player's Isolation Barrier would disappear and leave an area defenseless upon reaching its limit. However, an argent's Fence instead assembled a mass of hexagons and distributed its endurance across each section. As long as the angel didn't run out of MP, she could easily fix the barrier, even if one section was pierced.

At first, any monster to escape the Fence was likely suppressed by the angel army. Opus had stopped by on occasion to maintain and restore the barrier as well as to supply additional MP, but they had used up most of this over the years and were almost at their limit. As a result, monsters scattered across the continent to become the bane of Cayna's existence.

"And the goblin army just now?"

"I apologize. I have my hands full overseeing the Fence, and..."

"Nah, I took care of them, so it's all good. Are you okay, though? Do you feel sick?" Cayna asked worriedly.

The argent's body flickered with static noise. It was a miracle she'd held on this long.

"You're...going to vanish soon, right?" Cayna said.

"Correct. I cannot last much longer."

"Couldn't I just give you a bunch of MP?"

The argent shook her head forlornly. "I do not even have enough strength to repair the Fence anymore. I have grounded my existence in every way I know how, and this is my limit."

"I see. Do you know what's going on inside?"

"Yes. The most vigorous have already escaped, but many are building their strength in anticipation. The moment it is clear Fence has lost its functionality, they will unleash their pent-up resentment and trample the outside world."

"It won't break down in the next two or three days, right?"

"Correct. I can still last for a few days, but it is very likely there will be impatient monsters who escape beforehand."

"Oh dear."

"The camp will go bye-bye," mumbled Kuu, who had remained silent so far. She looked back toward the direction of the camp.

"Are there normal people in the vicinity?" the argent asked.

"The only one who can fight is Cohral. At level 300, it'll be tough for him to defend a group of fifty… But Exis and Quolkeh are there, too, so maybe it's fine?"

"Unlike the local monsters, the ones from that world can sharply perceive foes. They will quickly detect a group of people nearby."

"Shoot, we better evacuate everyone fast. We'll have to evoke martial law in the capital, too. I'm sure Opus will figure something out, so hang in there."

Cayna turned around to leave but first asked the shubez what it planned to do.

"I will spy among the monsters inside."

"Huh. I don't really get it, but do your best, too."

After giving a light wave good-bye, Cayna hurried back to camp and explained to the faculty and adventurers that a monster attack was almost imminent.

"Last time the knights were useless while we adventurers drove 'em away. What's the issue?"

Jild had apparently been present at some point during the earlier attack when a game monster controlled the monsters of this world. They had managed to fend them off somehow, but the adventurers would be crushed like pebbles by the roadside if game monsters were the main force. Cohral and Exis, the latter of whom had stealthily joined the rest of the adventurers, helped convince Jild that this was a dangerous tactic.

"Nonetheless, we cannot move at night," said one of the Academy faculty members. "Do you mind if we at least wait until morning?"

After conferring with the student representatives, the teachers refused to budge on this point. Cayna accepted.

"Still, the Abandoned Capital? What kinda crazy monsters are sealed up in there…?" Exis wondered aloud.

"How am I supposed to know?" asked Cayna.

"I see. Hey, that ghost ship must've been from the Abandoned Capital, too. Let's avenge Luka's village."

"It's fine that you're itching for a fight, but hold on a sec."

"Why?"

"Opus is planning an event just for this occasion. Granted, I don't actually know if it's a quest or event, though."

"So, that guy is up to somethin' again… You better keep a tight rein on him."

"He's slippery as an eel!"

Meanwhile, Opus spoke in the nameless darkness.

"All right, my preparations are complete. It looks like Cayna has been brought up to speed as well. And so begins the final quest."

He flashed a wicked smile and set things in motion.

CHAPTER 4

An Announcement, an Assembly, an Event, and a Beginning

The day after Cayna met with the argent and the shubez, she sent the students back to the capital. A number of participants were naturally upset that their outing had lasted only one day, and complaints rose from the adventurers who had been forced to abandon their request as well.

"There's no reason to panic over a horde of monsters that might not even come!" Jild shouted at Cayna in front of the Adventurers Guild.

Cayna, however, remained perfectly calm. "You're free to take the lead and die, but don't shoot the messenger."

Whatever questions everyone had about the sealed quest monsters, Cayna couldn't just peek inside the Abandoned Capital. This meant she didn't have the whole picture. Nonetheless, as far as Cayna knew, even the smallest shrimp in there could eat Jild for breakfast. He was well aware of her pitying gaze and reasonably angered by it.

As Cohral watched in silence, he decided Cayna's attitude was unhelpful and stepped between them.

"Relax," he said.

"Ngh," Jild grunted. "Fine."

"Cayna is worried about you in her own way. She might not look it, but that girl is the strongest person here right now. Still, I agree she's got a sharp tongue and just blurts whatever is on her mind."

"What, that pip-squeak?!"

Both Jild and fellow adventurers in the guild who had been listening in glanced back at Cayna incredulously. If Cayna herself had claimed this, only about half would have believed her. The Armor of Victory had been active in Felskeilo's Adventurers Guild for many years, and a long string of successes lent their words credibility.

"She's stronger than you, Supreme Swordsman?" Jild asked Cohral.

"Hmm?"

"Are you saying even you're no match for this little lady?"

"Exactly. I understand you have expectations of me, but I'd be dead in an instant if I challenged her. When it comes to raw strength, Cayna can't be beat."

"…Oh yeah? Got it."

Jild had expected a different answer, but he backed down the second Cohral admitted he was weaker than Cayna.

"I feel like I messed up somehow…," said Jild.

"If you talk like a player, only other players will get it," Cohral explained. "No matter what you say, no one else will understand. Just accept it."

"Yep," said Cayna. "Thanks for stepping in, Cohral."

"No problem. It's the least I can do!"

Pleased by Cayna's kind praise, Cohral thumped his chest. After pledging to lend their aid, his party members followed Jild and the Swift Horses.

"I do not know your intentions, but your cut will be temporarily reduced once everything is over, Cohral," the Armor of Victory's leader warned with a humorless smile.

"Seriously?!"

"Yes, seriously."

Cohral's shoulders slumped.

"Um, my condolences...?" Cayna offered.

"...*Sigh*."

Upon the group's return to Felskeilo, Cayna reached out to Mai-Mai and Skargo. She also sent a letter to Kartatz saying that this was an urgent matter.

Skargo quickly said he would advise the king, so it seemed each of her children was informed without issue.

Afterward, Cayna summoned a Green Dragon and sent it off to deliver a letter to Sahalashade in Otaloquess. It concerned the previous night's discussion about the Abandoned Capital barrier.

She also tried contacting Opus via a Friend Message, but he had yet to respond. He was the one who first told her to go to the barrier, so Cayna figured it was only right that he be kept in the loop about the event. Her patience had long since worn thin.

"Sheesh. What's that jerk up to...?"

"How should I put this, Mother? You've been speaking rather poorly of Uncle Opus for a while now..."

"He's not twiddling his thumbs at times like these! Trust me, I speak from experience! Opus is a nutcase even in the heat of battle."

Beside her was Mai-Mai, who had received Cayna's message and addressed the students. After notifying everyone that the event would be held another day, Mai-Mai remained behind.

Her mother had been searching for a private, spacious area to converse with her fellow players, so Mai-Mai proposed the Academy campus. Cayna took her up on this offer and changed venues to pick up where they left off.

The tactics of that despicable Opus often exploited the guild members and players of his own nation. For example, in wartime he would draw over 80 percent of enemy fire to the boundary line and initiate an event that inundated the area with monsters. Cayna and two other guild members, however, were roped into defending the main base in the meantime. After summoning a wall of dragons and fighting over a thousand players for four straight hours, the trio spent the rest of the day exhausted.

The fear players felt for this heinous event was indescribable, as it enveloped them in a darkness no skill could penetrate and unleashed a constant wave of monsters. Since enemy players had a respawn point in the area, participants spent the remaining half of the day in an endless cycle of revival and death. Of course, players from opposing nations who knew the culprit continued to bash Opus in the forums.

Opus and his crew would also cast Disguise in advance and sneak into the Red Kingdom, which didn't even share a border with the Black Kingdom. In the last ten minutes of the battle, they'd fire off Meteorite Drop: Giga Strike (with Buff as a cherry on top) near the boundary line. The long-range attack blasted bitter rivals blue and red indiscriminately.

Since the rule had always been that the Collection Point belonged to whichever nation controlled it in the last ten minutes of battle, the Black Kingdom's success auspiciously brought it under their possession.

Both official and fan forums later exploded, and the resulting chaos pushed the Admins into a corner. They responded several days later, and needless to say, they modified the rules for occupation.

Thinking back on it, Cayna couldn't help but feel she'd been sent on a suicide mission for that very purpose. Of course, she jumped right in, despite the unfavorable odds that had been made clear to her. However, this was purely because she'd been talked into it. Opus's silver tongue was matched only by the former sub-leader, Ebelope.

More than old fury, Cayna felt a sense of exhaustion and misery each time this memory resurfaced. Mai-Mai misunderstood her silence as something dreadful, and she paled.

"Don't go diggin' up painful old memories," Exis begged Cayna.

"Sounds to me like you got roped in, too, Tartar Sauce," she replied.

"I told you, it's not Tartarus now, either!"

Quolkeh stood next to him looking conflicted, and on his other side was Ark, smiling brightly. With a girl on each arm, he attracted the bloodshot, murderous gazes of every lovestruck fool in the vicinity but brushed these aside like a gentle breeze. Male jealousy was no match for the Cream Cheese guild's rigorous mental training.

"Not exactly sure where you came from, but it looks like you sniffed out my location," said Cayna.

"What are you talking about?" Exis demanded. "It's easy to figure out a friend's location if you've got a proper map."

"Huh? It is...?"

Exis had trekked across every corner of the continent as an adventurer, so his world map was pretty much complete—unlike Cayna's, which was spotty, since she traveled only between the major cities and the main road to the east.

"He had the gall to hide from me that he can teleport," Quolkeh grumbled.

"Hey, look—you always want an ace up your sleeve, right? You never know what might happen," Exis countered.

"You could've at least said *something*…"

Anyone who didn't know the pair would easily mistake this exchange for a lovers' quarrel.

"Ah, I get it," said Cayna. "You jumped to the closest spot and then made a beeline for me."

Exis had registered the destroyed fishing village, Luka's home, on his map just in case. He and Quolkeh had used travel-based skills to pass through forests and rivers but were attacked by goblin soldiers once they were near Cayna's location. They ran into her just after launching a counterattack.

"Ark," said Cayna.

"Yes?"

"This guy is your brother, right?"

"Yes. His face got a bit nastier, but he's definitely Tar-Tar."

"…Tar-Tar?"

"Oh! Um, that was my nickname for his old avatar. It didn't mesh well in real life, though. One day I just started calling him that…" Ark waved her hands in a frantic effort to explain, which charmed everyone except Exis, who sank into despair.

"This is just how dragoids look," he muttered.

"Right, right. It's been ages, Tar-Tar. Glad to see you're still… your usual self. Plus, you seem to be doing well."

Ark was now so calm and composed that one had to wonder why she'd been so nervous before. Cayna was visibly shocked.

"………I totally forgot she's like this…," Exis moaned. He heaved a deep sigh and slumped his shoulders dejectedly.

Cayna remembered how everyone in the Cream Cheese guild took digs at Tartarus to get a funny reaction out of him; this must have been a daily occurrence in real life as well. She could under-stand making a separate account to escape his bullies in both the game and reality, but it was still a mystery why he didn't hang up his controller.

"Gee, you're so strong and fierce now that I hardly recognized you," Ark told him.

"Drop it already!"

The two were left alone to reestablish (?) their sibling bond.

Quolkeh, who had been brought up to speed on Exis's situation along the way, watched the scene with amusement.

With Exis and Ark's joyful reunion now out of the way, Cayna seamlessly switched to the topic at hand: joining forces.

"You guys made the mistake of coming here, but that actually works in my favor, so help a girl out, please and thanks."

"You really couldn't put that any nicer, huh?" asked Quolkeh.

"I'd say you've got it pretty good if this much absurdity is throw-ing you for a loop."

"You mean it gets worse?!"

"Don't start with her, Quolkeh," Exis cautioned. "Even back in the guild, Cayna was a special brand of absurdity."

"Um, could you not lump me together with Opus and Ebelope?"

"You're exactly as bad as they are! Just in a different way!"

"Whaaa?!"

""She's legit surprised…?"" Quolkeh and Cohral muttered in exasperation. This confirmed their suspicions that top-level guild members were a different breed of odd.

Mai-Mai, meanwhile, stood by idly, no longer able to follow the conversation.

Kuu tugged on Cayna's ear and urged her to get back on topic. "The Abandoned Capital! The Abandoned Capital!"

Finally, Cayna remembered what she wanted to say and pressed a palm to her fist. "Anyway, I wanted to ask you guys to help exterminate the Abandoned Capital's monsters. How about it?"

She made this sound like a leisurely monster hunt. Her fellow players shared the same sentiment:

""""That's a job for a Skill Master! Keep us out of this!!"""""

Cohral, Quolkeh, and Exis vehemently shot her down, but Ark appeared clueless. Since they'd be involved, Cayna explained the growing monster situation and how the argent's Fence was on its last leg.

"Don't turn your back on a fellow player," Cayna urged. "Although I'll admit there's a good chance you'll end up in the line of fire. Could you at least help me clean up the chumps that slip through the cracks?"

"Hmm. The Abandoned Capital's pretty massive, though. It might be dilapidated, but it was still the capital of the Brown Kingdom. You say the place is infested with monsters—how many monsters are we talkin' here?" asked Exis.

"He's got a point," said Quolkeh. "It's impossible for the four of us. We don't even know what levels these monsters are."

Back in the game, each of the seven capitals arbitrarily became starter areas for new players. Thanks to this, one purpose they served was to provide support and a suitable place to buy beginner weapons and items.

Moreover, materials harvested on individual hunts found their way to player-run vendors that specialized in item production. Each region was different, and there was a myriad of local specialties.

In addition, sprawling dungeons were typically built underground, so midlevel players (around level 500) could play along the capitals' outskirts. These might be subterranean waterways, an ancient city buried beneath the foundation, a secret base built by some magician as a hobby, or a research facility sealed away after a chemical accident. The backstory changed with each city.

The worst among these was the Black Kingdom, which was constantly overflowing with riches. Deep in an underground cavern, descendants of a demon king apparently kept an eagle eye on the world above and sought to rule it. Needless to say, the nation was not friendly to novices in any capacity.

Sure enough, this was the root of Exis's concerns. A monster infestation on the surface was one thing, but if there was an underground facility beneath the capital, it could swell to three times that number. How could a few players eliminate all the enemies crammed down there?

Of course, Cayna was a *Leadale* addict like Exis/Tartarus and had taken this into account as well.

"I bet their levels run the gamut," Cayna said.

"C'mon, take this seriously! How can four people handle somethin' like that?"

"We'll have Opus, too. Plus it's not like we can just sit around and do nothing. I don't want to imagine any more kids ending up orphaned like Luka, so I've been using my connections to sound out the defenses of all three nations."

"...Maybe you've been at this for a while," started Quolkeh, "but the fact you can ask each government for help blows my mind..."

Cayna smiled uncomfortably. For whatever reason, the Foster Children and relatives she encountered were deeply involved in various state affairs. Most of them were too busy to travel abroad, due to their positions. Mai-Mai, who stood grinning in front of Cayna, was no exception.

"How did things turn out this way...?" Cayna asked.

"It is because of your personal virtue, Mother!"

"What virtue is that? I was gone for two hundred years. It makes zero sense..."

The whole situation made her want to sigh. This was soon accompanied by a piercing howl from above.

A Black Dragon with massive wings and a body the size of a gymnasium skidded to a halt. It was level 550. In terms of the Summoning Magic: Dragon spell, it boasted unmatched strength like the Red Dragon but also specialized in long-range magic. Cayna had often called upon it in times of war. Then, two people alighted from its back. The first was Opus, who wore a pure black coat. The second was his constant maid Siren.

"Please forgive our tardiness, Lady Cayna," said Siren.

"You're still hanging around here?" Opus teased.

"Uncle Opus?"

"Damn it, Opus!" Exis shouted.

"Wow, two Skill Masters in one place," said Cohral. "Wonders never cease..."

"That's terrifying somehow," quipped Quolkeh.

Mai-Mai, Exis, Cohral, and Quolkeh each felt a strange premonition in turn and made their thoughts known. Cayna alone furrowed her brow in concentration.

A collaboration between Leadale's Kongming and the Silver Ring Witch struck fear into the hearts of Cohral and Quolkeh, and Exis likewise shivered at the thought of such an alliance coming together on the eve of a decisive battle.

Before anyone had a chance to speak, the momentary silence was interrupted by a massive human figure floating in the sky.

Suddenly, it appeared directly over not only the Academy but also the entire capital. Something brighter than the sun glittered in the cloudless sky. Back in the castle, Shining Saber immediately prepared to unsheathe his blade but moved no further.

It wasn't just the inhabitants of the castle—every citizen across the city stared up in disbelief. This was an inevitable reaction, considering the immense scale. No citizen, traveler, adventurer, merchant, or wanderer was exempt as everyone continued to watch incredulously.

The figure was concurrently visible in both Otaloquess and Helshper and also appeared above villages scattered across every region. It bewildered every corner of the continent.

Queen Sahalashade froze as she handed a response letter to Cayna's Green Dragon. In Helshper, Caerina and the king glanced out the window. And in the remote village, everyone noticed something was off and raced out of their homes. No matter one's location, it was impossible to miss.

A smiling angel of ethereal beauty sported a pair of white wings and held a lithograph in one hand. Divine light illuminated it from behind, and most fell to their knees in prayer at the very sight. Only a minuscule percentile failed to react, simply because they'd met the angel before.

"I come bearing a message."

The angel's androgynous, melodic voice echoed in the minds of all who gazed upon it. There was a long pause after the first sentence, but the next was something vastly unfamiliar to the people of this continent.

"The Leadale Administration would like to notify all players about the final event."

Cayna and the other players knew this angel perfectly well.

Exis, Quolkeh, Cohral, and Ark heard it countless times back in the day and glared at the messenger high above them. Only Mai-Mai seemed nervous. Cayna tiredly watched Opus gloat over his own success. She slumped her shoulders. There was nothing more to say now that he'd gotten the ball rolling.

"In a few days' time, the large barrier surrounding the Abandoned Capital will unravel."

Anyone in a position of national importance jolted at the name.

"It is the duty of all players to eliminate the monsters that will overrun the capital."

Beneath the distant sky, Luvrogue looked up and remembered the sensation that had encircled his neck until recently. He clenched his fist.

In his floating garden, a certain dwarf stood dressed in full armor. He took one swing of a battle halberd taller than himself and then gazed at the blue sky.

"We Administrators anticipate each of you to accomplish your duty to the fullest. May you be victorious."

The angel repeated this message once more and dissipated into the air. Only the unsettled citizens who continued to crane their necks were proof it ever existed.

Back in the remote village, a teary-eyed Luka clung to Roxine's skirt.

"Mommy Cayna...," she whispered.

*   *   *

Then, in a certain village:

"H-hold it right there, you. Why'd you suddenly take out that old thing?" Camy asked harshly. She worked at the only tool shop in town.

Her husband started to don the equipment he wore when they first met. It was a full suit of armor and a large sword, and she had to wonder where he'd been storing it in the house all this time. He had it on the day he unexpectedly appeared with a lost look on his face. Unbelievably, there wasn't a single scratch or even a speck of dust on either the armor or the sword.

"Oh, sorry, sorry," he told his wife. "It looks like I've gotta step out for a bit."

His casual tone suggested he was going to stop by the neighbor's to borrow farm equipment, but her husband's back held some kind of resolve.

Camy had been running their household for several decades, but his unfamiliar behavior confused her. No, it was the same when they'd first met long ago and her husband took on a mission to vanquish a monster spotted near the village.

"I have to leave for a few days, but I'll be home soon. No need to worry."

He patted their child's head soothingly, and his wife looked up at him with a sense of déjà vu.

The soldier with the childlike smile stood before her once again. He had become a bearded, middle-aged man in the blink of an eye, but Camy hid this teary-eyed nostalgia with a smack to her husband's face.

"Ack?!"

"Hmph! Business will plummet while you're gone, so just hurry back already!"

"Sheesh… Where did the simple young girl I once knew go?"

"Quit your blabbering and get a move on!"

"Ow, ow, ow, ow! Okay, okay, I'll see you later."

The husband chuckled as he dodged his wife's pestle stick and dashed outside. After lightly waving to her through the window, he took a stone from his inside pocket (an item he'd saved for an emergency event) and crushed it in his hand. His wife watched as he transformed into an arrow of light and flew toward the western sky. She clasped her hands together and prayed to a deity unrelated to the angel hovering above the village in the afternoon sky.

Then, at the entrance to a certain forest…

"Well, I'm off."

"Do take care."

A youthful-looking female elf and an older elf conversed. The black-haired woman was dressed in leather armor and carried both a rapier and short wand at her side for the journey ahead. Seeing her off was an old elf in emerald robes whose white beard came down to his waist. Slightly pointed ears distinguished the two as high elves, and these woods were the only link to their home in the Verdant Forest.

"If you meet one of our kind, can you tell them to return to the forest?"

"It will depend on their stubbornness. I'll extend an invitation, but please don't be upset if no one comes."

"I suppose it can't be helped until the next opportunity…"

"They'll hate us if we're too persistent."

The two were like grandfather and granddaughter as they enjoyed each other's company. Then, the old high elf smiled and turned around. He cast Forest Knocker and disappeared through the doorway.

"*Sigh*. My goodness. There's always so much to do whenever I come out here," the high elf girl mumbled tiredly after watching him leave.

She took a stone from her inner pocket and crushed it. An instant later, her body transformed into an arrow of light and arced across the sky.

Then, in western Helshper...

"Ah, you there. Stop what you're doing for a moment!"

"Huh?"

After obtaining permission from Caerina and the knight captain, Luvrogue stepped away from his duties and headed outside town. He'd apparently been staring up at the heavenly angel with a serious expression, and his inexplicable request was swiftly accepted.

He left from the western gate and traveled along the main road, but a voice called out just as he gripped the stone in his hand. Luvrogue turned around and saw a young werecat man race toward him with one arm raised. He clattered and clanged in heavy metallic armor, a rarity for the race.

"Phew. Thank goodness I found a comrade. You're a player, aren't you?"

"Yeah, I'm Luvrogue. I'm guessing you're a player, too?"

"Yes, yes, I'm Hernel. I've run out of emergency teleportation items and would really appreciate it if you took me with you."

"Got it. I'll request to form a party, so just confirm it."

"Thanks."

Both checked their own windows and registered the party. Once this was done, Hernel breathed a sigh of relief.

"Can you believe the Admins suddenly gave us an emergency mission? I didn't even think anyone still had that authority here."

For Luvrogue, the word *Admins* brought only one person to mind. His assumption was correct, but the authority of a Game Master automatically meant a connection to the Administrators in the mind of an average player like himself. He'd met only one Game Master so far, but her words and actions confirmed another was involved.

"I only know one person with the power of a Game Master."

"What? Really?! This is the first time I've heard of a Cream Cheese member in this world. Did you meet them, Luvrogue?"

"...I met a witch."

"Ack! I-I'm glad you're okay..."

For beginner to average players like Luvrogue and Hernel and even addicts, anyone called by a nickname was like TNT. He had learned his place and almost died after picking a fight with one. Luvrogue couldn't say this, however, and remained ambiguous.

"Y-yeah, I guess...," he replied with a stiff smile.

Hernel seemed to read something in his expression. He gave Luvrogue a comforting pat on the shoulder and said, "No worries."

Such concern from a fellow otherworlder was a first for Luvrogue, and his eyes misted as he crushed the stone in his hand.

And now, let us return to our original scene.

Opus's preferred encampment was located on Felskeilo's main road and intersected the outer trade routes that ran down the continent's northern and southern coastlines. A steel tower that acted as a parabolic antenna was stationed along the very edge of the roadside. Back in the Game Era, this was an antenna receiver for teleportation stones during emergency missions.

Incidentally, Mai-Mai wanted to participate but was left behind since this was both a player event and potentially fatal. Ark was a player, and she also declined, since meeting other players would be awkward, given her rare weapon. She felt pretty guilty, but Exis and his sister complex insisted he could fight for both of them and made her stay back.

"This was built by the Admin spies who hid among the players, right?" Cayna murmured as she looked up at the tower.

"There were several others besides me," said Opus.

Such was the general opinion of those who understood the situation.

After a short while, several player lights flew in from the south, east, and north and landed near the steel tower. Previous arrivals took charge and received the trickle of newcomers. Temporary parties were then created based on level and whether one was a vanguard or rear-guard. This swift action was no different from back in the day. After all, any group of players was always eager to show off.

At present, participating players were separated by party but connected by the function known as Raid Link. If any one person cast wide-range defensive magic, everyone would receive those benefits. Nonetheless, this would also require the proper amount of MP.

"Still," said Cayna, "we don't even have thirty people…"

"A siege attack is out of the question. Our best bet is to rush in and trample the monsters while the barrier holds," Opus suggested.

A White Dragon the size of a five-story building held a scrap of wood that said STRATEGY HQ in its mouth while Cayna, Opus, and two other players brainstormed beneath it. Cayna had summoned the dragon earlier. In fact, she and Opus had summoned seven level-990 dragons just to be on the safe side.

The Green Dragon sent to Otaloquess on Cayna's orders had delivered her letter and returned with Queen Sahalashade's response. She sent it away for a moment before resummoning the dragon at maximum level. Each dragon was an expert assistant in its own way and proved quite useful.

The White Dragon specialized in full recovery magic, while the

Black and Red Dragons excelled in attack magic. The Blue Dragon couldn't move on land, but Cayna could summon it in water to unleash a massive tsunami. The Brown Dragon could cross any terrain and defensewise was a cut above the rest. The Green Dragon had giant wings and, although slow on land, was an excellent flier. Its wind-based Assistance Magic was highly useful as well. The Violet Dragon looked like a giant purple toad with horns, a tail, and small wings. However, its poisonous breath could strike the enemy with a number of status ailments.

Despite their vast differences in abilities, these dragons could improve the outcome of battle whenever they acted solo. Now that Cayna and Opus were together, they had the added bonus of perpetual, unrestricted summonings.

"It's great to have some Limit Breakers around," Jaeger said.

"Still, I must admit it took years off my life when I saw you both together," Spirale replied.

The middle-aged human man dressed entirely in red armor was the player Jaeger. Back in the game, he was an influential player, a citizen of the Red Kingdom, and the leader of the Silver Watches guild. It was said to be the largest in *Leadale* with over two thousand members, and they dominated both group-based Mission Quests and attack-based Story Quests. His typical position was an active level-800 vanguard.

There was also the blue dragoid Spirale who wore robes and carried a wand. He was level 800 as well and excelled as a rearguard. Although this eccentric specialist chose a vanguard-type race, he brought together his fellow oddball players (librarians who could find any book, dwarfs who spent their entire game lives digging holes, cliff denizens, et cetera) to create the Archive Alley guild and serve as its leader. Even within the game, the information network that spawned from this collection of quirky experts became a prime source of content.

"The problem is what's inside, right?" Cayna asked.

"Huh? It's not like the Underworld or Hermit areas got mixed up in this world. They might be tough, but I'd peg 'em at no higher than level 600," replied Jaeger.

"Dear me, no," said Spirale. "The Demon King's descendants are on this continent as well. If we run into them, it'll be no laughing matter…"

"Ah, the ones beneath the Black Kingdom? You fought those irritating maggots? I wasn't aware they made it here," Opus said.

"Right, I heard about 'em. Don't they rule an underground labyrinth?"

"When I was around level 900, me, Ebelope, Meshmout, Tartarus, Straw Paper, and San annihilated them," Cayna explained. "You might call it a shaky win, though."

"If you had been destroyed at that level, I daresay no other player would have stood a chance."

"The heck?" said Jaeger.

Spirale listened with keen interest but frowned at the word *annihilated*.

"You won by takin' each other out?" Jaeger asked, his arms crossed.

Cayna shook her head and then looked down with a dark expression. "We thought all hope was lost and used a last resort."

"Ah, *that* last resort," Opus muttered to himself, nodding. "Yes, it makes sense…"

Everyone else eyed him curiously, and he calmly made eye contact with Cayna as if seeking permission to elaborate. She quickly agreed, so Opus carried on.

"She's talking about Special Skill: Self-Destruct," he said.

""Self-Destruct?!""

Jaeger had never heard of such a thing and jolted in surprise. Spirale knew of it but never felt the need to bother with the laundry list of skills needed to obtain it.

Of the many available long-range attack skills, Self-Destruct boasted the highest damage. However, its level of convenience depended on the user's stats. Such power was calculated by experience points until level-up x (user level + remaining HP/MP), so if someone high-level like Cayna used it, the results would be obvious.

Unfortunately, in addition to death, the caster also went down a level. And since the skill didn't discriminate, Cayna wiped out all her party members who were already on the brink of death. Everyone eventually respawned, but since her level also determined the diameter of the attack dome, most of the players in the Black Kingdom capital directly above the dungeon were caught up in the blast and died as well.

The subjugation party kept mum on the matter, so the Sudden Death in the Black Kingdom Capital Incident became one of *Leadale*'s many mysteries. Aside from Cayna and her fellow guild members, only the Admins ever knew the truth.

"Those were fixed monsters instead of event ones, so the two won't mingle here...or so I hope." Opus offered an educated guess, since he couldn't just say that he was the one who assembled everyone.

In truth, even he didn't know how many Event Monsters awaited them. This was because he had put a marker on the Event Monsters' spawn point and connected everything to the Abandoned Capital regardless of whether their numbers were multiplying. He then left the rest to the summons, so whatever monster ecosystem had formed inside afterward was a mystery.

Since Opus couldn't announce this publicly, his predictions were set aside and the conversation continued.

"Everyone arrived here at different times, so they've gotten acclimated over the years. A battle might be a tall order," Jaeger insisted.

Several players listening nearby nodded in agreement. Some had invited fellow players who had been in this world longer to join the fight, but lingering attachments kept them from participating. Indeed, when Cayna considered a future where Luka survived her, it wasn't hard to understand how they felt. Jaeger himself had friends and family waiting back home, so personal motivations varied in that regard.

"As a guild leader, I'm used to lookin' after a large group. Think of me like as a student council president," Jaeger insisted.

"Don't council members have to do endless chores around the school? No waaaay," said Cayna.

"But my subordinates were brilliant. For the most part, everyone, including the guild sub-leader, had my back and followed every order."

"There's a limit to outsourcing," Opus remarked.

"Heyyyy. Got a report for ya."

"Great work, Exis."

The slightly dirtied dragoid approached them. He had formed a small party currently keeping watch over the entrance in shifts. The argent's absence from the Abandoned Capital was already evident. This was because Opus had called off the summons after Cayna cast an Isolation Barrier over Fence's perimeter. With the front of the city as the sole entrance and exit, the group could eliminate any monsters that broke through.

"How's the situation?" Cayna asked Exis.

"We have more hands now, so things have gotten a bit easier. But like you said, the systemized dinosaur and mage-type monsters haven't shown up yet. Almost all of 'em are average quest monsters between levels 200 and 300. On top of that, they're coming at us in spurts instead of all at once."

A manageable crowd meant they could take down whatever monsters came first and figure out how to deal with the rest. Every player in the area was Raid Linked at present, so despite a slight ratio shift, everyone would receive a small bit of experience each time even one person defeated an enemy. However, some were no doubt disgruntled by the value difference between those fighting on the field and those not. Upon hearing about this, players had raced here to test their mettle.

Although masters of Revival Magic were on call, they cautioned Exis to exercise restraint, since there was no guarantee such spells would work.

Exis assembled everyone who wished to join the front lines and led them back down the road from whence he came. Half of their forces left to thoroughly block off the entrance.

"The Great Kongming is a pro at this kind of thing, right?" remarked Jaeger.

"What? No chance," said Cayna. "Opus is all about scheming and waiting in the wings. In fact, sneak attacks are his go-to. There aren't paid items here, either, so either way we're in for a tough fight. Our guild pretty much depended on our levels to carpet-bomb everything in sight during party battles. I guess you could call that a strategy?"

Jaeger and Spirale heaved a collective sigh.

They had been together constantly except in wartime, and someone like Cayna, who could join a party without any need for backup, was quite the asset. If she focused solely on attack *and* her guild fought as one, it was a recipe for destruction.

Tell me something I don't know..., thought Jaeger and Spirale.

Opus, aka *Leadale*'s Kongming, naturally had expectations of his own. However, he was the type to hide away and refine his strategy prior to battle. He had calmly taken everything into account and understood not to get his hopes up.

"Hmm. Looks like they're carrying out a standard assault tactic. What if we restructure our parties to match the enemy's level?" suggested Jaeger.

"Our midlevel players are already in the vanguard. The rearguard is hurting, correct?" Spirale pointed out.

Cayna chimed in. "In other words, we're thin in the back. Too thin."

"That's because the winds will later shift in favor of the vanguard. The monsters might drop all sorts of useful items," replied Opus.

"Who the hell thought up a hand grenade? That's definitely from another game," Jaeger grumbled, citing an unrelated robot title set in a dystopian future.

Spirale opened the current party link in his window and alongside Jaeger commanded each player to reorganize.

The current HQ consisted of these four, but Opus and Cayna remained in the rearguard so they could play it by ear no matter the situation. Both could have stood on the front lines if they choose but stuck to the back after the other players' quest for glory implied disapproval. Jaeger and Spirale acted as the vanguard's command center while Opus led the rearguard, so everyone reached an understanding.

"What will you do, Cayna?" Jaeger asked.

"Um, obviously I'll aid everyone from behind with Buffs."

"I understand, but friendly fire is still a possibility," said Spirale. "Please do not blow away our allies with long-range magic."

"Just who do you think I am, Spirale?"

"An incarnation of destruction."

"......"

Cayna fell into silent disappointment as their surroundings erupted into laughter, but several sensed her wrath and quickly backed away in fear. The main reason ordinary players (?) wanted to fight at the front was due to the level of monsters back in the game. After all, aside from several special areas, an enemy's level was 600 max. There were a few quest exceptions, of course, but the Limit Breakers could rush in like some corrupt politician's bodyguard if need be.

"Ahhhhh?!?!"

There was a sudden yell, and every bewildered player who heard it turned toward the source. A black-haired high elf woman had just alighted beneath the receiver tower and pointed at Cayna and yelped in surprise.

Cayna recognized her immediately.

"Oh..."

"Ah."

As did Opus. Cayna started smiling, but the demon's expression went blank.

The woman dashed up to Cayna but face-planted in the ground at her feet when Opus tripped her.

For a moment, no one made a sound. Some flinched at Opus's violent act while others showed concern for the high elf now motionless on the ground. The culprit held his stomach in uncontrollable laughter.

After a few seconds, the woman's head shot up. Her expression was a mix of joy and sadness as tears poured like waterfalls from her eyes.

"Sissyyy!" she cried.

"Wait—are you okay, Sahana? Stop doing that every single time, Opus..."

Some shocked onlookers started criticizing Opus's behavior. They couldn't believe he did this every time and gazed with compassion as Cayna helped the woman back up. After brushing away the dust and tears, Sahana squeezed her tightly. Anyone would assume this was a reunion between sisters, though it was Sahana who appeared older.

"Spirale, I've got someone perfect for the rearguard," said Cayna, still in her little sister's arms.

"She's from the high elf community, right? We should be fine now."

Sahana was a former member of the high elf community. Tall, with raven hair and eyes, she specialized in Assistance Magic. Back in their community days, Sahana devoted herself to Cayna to a troublesome degree and, at level 850, was a force to be reckoned with.

At the game's height, she and five others—each an average of level 800—formed one of the most outstanding and influential rearguard units in all of *Leadale*. The threat their support-only group posed was entirely unprecedented.

After a moment, Spirale explained the situation and party ratio to Sahana, and she gladly agreed to aid the vanguard. Everything went so well it was almost disappointing.

"Didn't think she'd say 'yes' right off the bat..."

"I wouldn't dare cause Cayna any trouble! I'm prepared to give this everything I've got!"

"This ain't the time for exaggeration. You must be outta your mind."

"We're not here to get carried away and burn the place to the ground."

"Goodness, don't assume I would ever disgrace my big sister."

"Don't get that look in your eye! You're not here for some sisterly skill slinging!"

Various players found Sahana's ardent dedication a bit disturbing.

"W-well, anything can happen. Just be careful, all right?" Cayna cautioned. "If you get overwhelmed at all, it's okay to leave the vanguard."

"Yes! I understand, Sissy!"

"I have my doubts…," Opus muttered.

"I don't want to hear that from you," Sahana replied with a murderous glare.

Opus was relieved to see this reunion didn't leave Sahana in blind ecstasy.

Then, Siren approached and bowed politely. "These appear to be the last for now."

"Right," replied Opus. "Good work."

"Wait, what?" said Cayna.

She stared in wonder at one of the four newcomers directly behind Siren: a demon in knight's armor. A well-armed werecat accompanying him raced over to Spirale.

"Leaderrrrrr!" the werecat cried.

"Buddyyy!"

He and Spirale immediately embraced.

"Hey, you made it," Cayna said to Luvrogue. "I wasn't sure if the knights would let you leave."

"I don't plan on dyin' here. I've still got stuff to do…," he muttered sorrowfully.

Cayna flicked his forehead. Sahana observed their familiarity with a death glare.

Although Luvrogue was a demon, he didn't appear to have any interest in Opus.

The humans and dragoid sulked when he didn't bother to greet them. *I guess we're just chopped liver,* they figured.

"I get why Cohral is here," Cayna began, "but what about you, Shining Saber? Can you step out like this?"

"...So, I'm a given? Getting my comrades to agree was no walk in the park, y'know," Cohral grumbled.

"For now I have permission from the king, plus my co-captain can handle things. A defensive fight should be no issue. Besides, you guys aren't gonna let those things escape the Abandoned Capital, right?"

Shining Saber directed that question at Cayna, but every player in earshot shouted, "Obviously!"

Shining Saber nodded. There were no definite rules, but eliminating those monsters was required to complete the quest. The players flown to this world were well aware of the tragedy that would occur if three-digit-level monsters escaped into the wild. He was pleased everyone felt the same way. After all, if a wave of monsters broke out here, Felskeilo would be their first victim.

"Well, let's get this extermination quest started," Jaeger told everyone in the Raid Chat.

The players responded with a rallying cry. This moment alone was bizarrely noisy, since she could hear the chat, but Cayna felt a slight sense of nostalgia and excitement.

Suddenly curious if Opus shared the sentiment, she looked next to her. However, he was staring at the receiver tower in keen bewilderment.

"What's wrong?" Cayna asked him.

"It's nothing. I just thought Hidden Ogre might come."

Now that he mentioned it, Cayna remembered Hidden Ogre was in this world, too. She'd heard that Exis had met him, but the dwarf apparently had no desire to see her. Everyone has their own circumstances, so Cayna didn't argue this.

"Come, let us begin our annihilation of the Abandoned Capital," Opus announced. "The plan will fail if Cayna is defeated. Know that if anything happens to her, you'll revert to regular people and be unable to use skills."

""""WHAAAAAAAAAAAAAAAAAAAAAAAAAAAT?!?!""""

As soon as Opus began his commencement speech, the players felt doomed.

"Don't start the battle with a bombshell!"

"Indeed. We haven't even discussed the reward yet."

""""Yeah! You tell 'em, Spirale!""""

At the mention of compensation, the other players cheered Spirale on. Material greed had seemingly won out.

Jaeger, the first to rouse his fellow players, promptly face-palmed. "Guess we've got other problems to deal with first..."

He glanced over at Cayna, the center of all this hubbub. Sahana was on the verge of tears and clinging to her.

"'If you die'?! Sissy, what does he mean?!"

"I'm not gonna die, so just relax."

"If anyone wishes you harm, I'll kill them! I'll even die in the process!"

"Hold it, hold it! No player would even try to pick a fight with me."

Just as her incoherent blubbering left Cayna at a loss, Kuu suddenly floated out and kicked Sahana in the forehead.

"Gyah?!" Sahana crumpled to the ground with an unladylike yelp.

"Kuu?!"

Cayna remembered that Kuu's kick always elicited the same response. It seemed to cause players significant pain.

Kuu had probably tinkered with the system to produce this effect. At any rate, Cayna used Search to check Sahana's status and confirmed a Faint effect. As she pressed a hand to her heart in relief and looked around, nearly everyone stood frozen in wide-eyed shock.

"Huh?" said Cayna.

Cohral and Shining Saber offered a strained smile. Cohral lightly pointed at Kuu, and she finally realized what was going on.

Even players rarely spotted fairies, which were mostly background characters in the Game Era. Once she remembered this, Cayna introduced Kuu to everyone.

"This is Kuu the fairy. She might not look it, but she's super violent. Make sure you leave a final will and testament before messing with her."

Several players who had always hoped fairies were real paled at her unsettling words.

Their kaleidoscope of emotions aside, Spirale glanced up.

"Something is falling!" he warned.

The players followed his gaze as round shapes whooshed overhead and blocked the sun.

"Parachutes?" one muttered.

"Huh? Maybe it's an aerial attack?"

"Are they monsters?"

"They wouldn't be that smart, right?"

"Demons or vampires could probably pull it off."

"Those can fly anyway!"

And so, the conversation derailed as approximately twenty people descended, one after the other. The parachutes disappeared to reveal a group of young girls and women.

"Ohhh!"

The men's eyes lit up in admiration, but several recipients looked down on them with disdain.

They seemed to be dressed in armor much like the players, and a small old man wearing a monk's *samue* garb brought up the rear. A cry of surprise rose from the crowd.

"""Hidden Ogre!"""

"Gramps?!"

"It's been a long while, Cayna."

The Twelfth Skill Master Hidden Ogre made a stylish entrance and saluted her.

All twenty of his little sisters had joined him. Since Foster Children couldn't use the item for emergency events, they had no choice but to move the floating Guardian Tower and parachute down.

"You still have twenty left?!"

"It's nothing compared to the one hundred and eight I had back in the good old days, but everyone is around level 500. They'll help out."

"To elevate this many to such a high level... Your sister complex is worse than I feared," Opus remarked.

The cheek of every player who had heard of the 108 foster sisters twitched, and they could only mumble in disbelief.

One of Hidden Ogre's sisters, a demon, immediately walked over to Cayna and gazed up at her with sparkling eyes. Such a fervent display of reverence baffled her. The girl was like a puppy wagging its tail.

"Ah, that is Yunio," said Lu Peixi. "She adores you, Lady Cayna."

"Come again?"

Despite the elf's succinct explanation, Cayna was still uncomprehending.

Hidden Ogre had evidently given his fifty-fourth sister, the demon Yunio, the flavor text *loves Cayna*.

"Why'd you write something like that, Gramps?"

"I ran out of ideas," was his heartfelt reply.

Cayna had no idea how to respond. As an experiment, she reached out and patted Yunio's head. The girl launched at her and gleefully pressed her head against Cayna's stomach. Unsurprisingly, Sahana shrieked from the shock.

"Even flavor text made it over here...?" one player said incredulously.

"Crap—I feel like I wrote some pretty crazy stuff, too!" wailed another.

A number of players who witnessed this scene trembled when they heard about the flavor text situation, but the girls were assigned to the rearguard. Jaeger wanted them on the front lines for their battle prowess, but he took the fact they were Foster Children into account and relegated them to the back. Incidentally, Hidden Ogre's level-800 stats meant he was put in the line of fire before he even had a chance to refuse.

"Players can use Revival Magic without a problem...but the success rate of foster kids and the people of this world are another story," muttered Spirale.

"Huh?" said Cayna. "Spirale, have you used Revival Magic since coming here?"

"Yeah, a number of times. It's extremely limited compared to the game, though."

"What? Really?"

Cayna wanted to know more details, but the event was about to start. Further questions would have to wait until later.

"Opus, you bastard. I'll make you explain more about the conditions for defeat later, but isn't there a reward for victory?" Cohral grumbled.

Several players then struck a fist against their palm in realization.

In the game, the reward for an emergency quest included a choice between experience points, a cosplay item with a slight bonus, or money.

"Hmm." Opus, the host of this event, mulled over this with a frown. It seemed this hadn't occurred to him, but now the players were riled up.

"Yeah, only a Game Master could call that notification angel, right?"

"Didn't the Limit Breakers have similar power?"

"It wasn't just about authority. Didn't some have connections to the Admins?"

"Oh yeah, there were totally Game Masters. I saw a knight in all red."

"Really? I saw someone who looked like a ghost."

"Okay, okay, quiet down!" Cayna called to the group, shooting Hidden Ogre and Opus a meaningful glance and a bright smile.

A clap echoed via a sound amplification spell, and everyone fell silent. Once their confused attention was on her, she grinned. Several people who knew her well enough sensed danger and stepped back. Indeed, the other players remained on edge as well. Cayna acted like this was no concern of hers and proposed a reward.

"In exchange for a successful quest, you'll get…two skills from us Skill Masters!"

"………………"

"""ALL RIIIIIIIIIIIIIIIIIIIGHT!!"""

After a brief silence, a wave of cheers broke out.

"Yeah! The Skill Masters sure are generous!"

"I can have the skills of my dreams!"

"The one I failed to get on that final day will finally be mine. It's been eating me up inside."

"Self-Destruct is every man's fantasy!"

"Don't go nuts. That's a death flag."

"Hmm. I'm content with my life now, so I don't need much."

"Something I could use on a daily basis would be nice."

Chatter and commotion erupted all at once.

"Well, that's the situation," said Cayna. "Much obliged, Gramps, Opus."

"I see. Are you fine with this, Hidden Ogre?" Opus asked.

"Ah, that's what you mean. If this turns out to be my last duty as a Skill Master, I've got no complaints."

As soon as Hidden Ogre granted his permission, the players buzzed with excitement.

"Okay, folks!" Jaeger boomed. "Exterminating every monster will spell victory! The fall of the Silver Ring Witch will spell our defeat! Gather your courage and fight!"

""""YEAAAAAAAAAAAAAH!!"""" came the players' rallying cry.

"Wish he wouldn't use the chaos just to say my nickname," Cayna grumbled.

"It was easier to understand that way, right?" Opus replied.

Spirale gave the order, and preparations for their annihilation quest began. Under his command, the players were divided into an assault unit and a dedicated support unit. There were just under thirty people in the former, Exis and his barrier observation team included. The latter had over forty.

"I think we might've broken the record for biggest rearguard."

"We've got a ton of foster kids, so nothin' for it."

Opus had rejected Lu Peixi's proposal to split her sisters into two groups and hold down the fort.

"Unlike warfare, our trouble won't end with the fall of the Capital," Opus said.

"Cayna can defend the stronghold, right?" Jaeger suggested. "We're toast if she's taken out."

"Thanks, no pressure there. Besides, I've got Kee and Kuu to protect me...," Cayna replied from nearby as everyone's hopeful gazes fell upon her. "And Yunio," she added.

"It would seem she's already grown on you," Opus noted.

"..."

His comment spoke for itself. As her friends' eyes grew tepid, Cayna summoned her Silver Ring to brush away the embarrassment. A large silver ring inset with seven orbs in every color of the rainbow circled her at waist level. Players who recognized it immediately began panicking.

"Why did you take that out all of a sudden, Sissy?!"

"What are we gonna do if you terrify our comrades?!"

Needless to say, Jaeger was immediately displeased.

The players pressed forward as one.

The former capital of the Brown Kingdom was unique in the fact it had a temple behind the castle. The town itself was spread out in a fan shape around the castle, and the roads connected like a mesh. The original landscape had surely been beautiful once, but none of the buildings along the streets had been left in any decent condition.

The group of dragons circling the city's walls overhead was a strange sight as well.

Cayna, Opus, Hidden Ogre, and Sahana worked together to summon this powerful squadron. Each member was no less than level 800.

The cobblestones were cracked and derelict with traces of shriveled-up weeds. Some areas had been stripped to reveal the bare

ground beneath, and there were huge, deliberate-looking holes everywhere. Like the buildings, not a single door or window remained intact. Everything had the tragic heroism of a horror game. An irritating odor would occasionally waft by on a warm breeze.

It wasn't just a scene that had broken down in a matter of a few months or years. There were fresh claw marks, and some buildings had been twisted apart by an incredible force.

"Wasn't this your magic's doing, Cayna?"

"How rude. It was rebuilt after the event, so this only happened in the past two hundred years."

"We still haven't found the culprits, though…"

"Maybe they went extinct on their own?" she suggested.

"Then none of us would have any reason to be here!"

Once someone spoke up, friendly conversation spread among the nervous players. They remained vigilant, but the silence was evidently unbearable.

"At any rate, this ground cleanup was definitely a rush job."

"The buildings are still standin' but look a mess. I bet they'd fall right over if you kicked 'em."

"Don't you dare. We'll get caught up in it!"

Since there were Skill Masters in the mix, it was suggested they take command. However, Hidden Ogre himself admitted a lack of leadership ability and declined. Cayna had the battle prowess and the authoritative skills but knew little of large-scale warfare, so Jaeger and Spirale were assigned the position as initially planned.

According to Exis and his team who had guarded the entrance, the monsters' sporadic escape attempts seemed to be on hold at the moment. However, they couldn't breathe easy yet, thanks to the earlier attack on Felskeilo.

Incidentally, Opus wasn't part of the conversation; he had gone underground by the entrance to hunt monsters in the subterranean tunnels. Siren did not join him but instead stood watch outside and explained the situation to any oblivious person who approached. Everyone was shocked when Opus announced he'd eliminate any foe on sight and destroy the tunnels as well.

"Hey, hey, hey, what are you planning?!" Exis had yelled at him.

"Once the tunnels collapse, the monsters will flood whatever exit they can find, right? All you have to do is strike there. It'll be like shooting fish in a barrel."

A number of players had nodded in understanding. Considering that it was a dungeon maze where monsters could pop out from anywhere, this was a reasonable proposal. Besides, the enemies aboveground took priority if they wanted to avoid a pincer attack.

If the objective had been simply to pulverize the city, Cayna and Opus could have used their strongest magic to get the job done in an instant. However, aside from a few exceptions, ranged spells fundamentally focused on the caster. Plus, unlike in the game, friendly fire was possible in this world. Magic couldn't automatically differentiate between a player and a nonplayer.

If they were to level the city with magic, only one person could enter. This was fine for either Cayna or Opus, but doing so would negate the entire point of assembling players for this emergency quest.

Opus's destructive activities were evidenced by the occasional slight tremor beneath the players' feet. The cobblestones from the town entrance onward slowly began to break down and collapse, so they had to keep moving.

"Better hope he doesn't get himself stuck," said Shining Saber, exasperated.

"I'm sure Opus has it covered. He's pretty smart about that stuff." Cayna vouched for the demon with a smirk.

"I see." Shining Saber nodded.

Just then, Kuu issued a warning from Cayna's shoulder: "Enemy!"

"Spirale, we've got company!" Cayna shouted. "Monster sighted!"

"Huh? What? Where?" Jaeger yelled once Cayna raised her magic staff and warned Spirale.

Without a moment's delay, the players on the front lines drew their weapons and stood on guard.

There was a fountain square in the center of town. The water had long since dried up, the earth was cracked, and shriveled weeds peeked out here and there.

"Are they underground?"

"Darn..."

"As I suspected, they're in a better position for an ambush."

The radar display of the Abandoned Capital was filled with countless red and blue dots that indicated friend or foe: blue for players, red for monsters. At present, the blue dots were gathered in the central plaza with a host of red dots circling them. The players had been simultaneously surrounded by the enemy.

Magic Skill: Physical Defense Up: Ready Set

Magic Skill: Magic Defense Up: Ready Set

Cayna's Buff spells immediately diffused everywhere and lit up the players in red and blue. Sahana added to this by casting Speed Up and Attack Power Up. The players were then cast in a green light, and their weapons glowed red.

Someone audibly gulped when suddenly one building in the direction of the castle exploded from the inside. Fragments of stone material and what looked to be broken furniture went flying.

Although everyone was well aware the physical defense boost would protect them, it is a normal instinct to dodge airborne objects.

Just as the panicked players either lay facedown on the ground or retreated, the buildings to the left and right exploded in the southern direction of their advance. The attack was clearly hostile, so they formed a vital circle to avoid an enemy strike from behind. The army had nearly recovered from the thick dust when something materialized from farther within.

It was a monster the size of a four-ton truck. The slimy toad had red and black spots, and a snake reared its head from the amphibian's partly open mouth.

"It's a chimera!"

""""Blegh...""""

As soon as one person perceived the monster's true nature, everyone else watched with annoyance. It wasn't alone, either; there was also an alligator with a shark's head and a two-headed Cerberus with the tail of a scorpion and heads of a snake and a dog. These monsters had no sense of unity whatsoever.

What appeared to be a rotund suit of armor came from the building on the left. However, at four meters tall, it was so huge one couldn't help but wonder where it had been hiding this whole time. When the living armor flipped up its helmet shield, a host of wriggling octopus legs flew out.

It was absolutely disgusting. A scream rose from the unit of little sisters.

Giant eyeballs substituted as the suit's joints, and it resembled an uneven, ball-jointed doll. The monster unsheathed not a sword from its side but a squirming, legless centipede. The corners of its mouth were wide enough to bite a person's head off in a single attack, and the slobber that trickled down was a dissolving solution that bored holes in the ground.

"I don't remember anything like *that* in the game!"

"Maybe it evolved in the barrier by itself for two hundred years?"

"This ain't the time for a casual analysis!"

Chimeras were relatively common monsters in *Leadale* and could often be found in ruins and dungeons. Their appearance was an amalgamation of two or three real-life animals, and apart from special areas, most players could beat one with ease as long as their physical attack was properly leveled up and the location was right.

What destroyed this balance was the troubled Admin design team who announced an open call for ideas in exchange for special items. Every passionate gamer artist, amateurs and pros alike, jumped at this with abandon. The design submissions alone were fine, but some players also included a list of detailed attack moves.

Furthermore, after the Admins carelessly accepted these with zero edits, violent monsters began to spread into newbie regions. *Leadale's* most powerful guilds later collaborated to launch a large-scale sweep. A majority of players at the time were upset, and the widespread propagation of chimera monsters came to an end.

"I guess only the most disgusting ones survived that extermination."

"Damn it! Is this another Admin trick?!"

"I know it's kinda late to say this, but the Admins' well of ideas ran dry a long time ago..."

"Stop, it just makes me sad."

Players who had memories of that cleanup job shot evasive looks at the armor and toad.

Both monsters were around level 300 and no match for the players here, but unfortunately it was no time for a counterattack. Other nearby buildings continued to explode, and the players' impatience became more pronounced as a stream of chimeras appeared one after the other. Despite their inferior strength, monsters of unknown ability surrounded them on all sides. This was enough to stop the army in its tracks.

Some players tried to move toward the wall, but another blast erupted in front of them. When they tried to shield themselves, another came from behind.

"Gaaah! Are they gonna keep us in this plaza?!" Jaeger shouted.

"Weird...," said Cayna. "I thought chimeras only acted on instinct."

Soon enough, the players were surrounded by a multitude of chimeras. Jaeger and Cayna, now both poised for battle, exchanged bewildered looks.

"What's going on? Are these monsters really smart enough to plan an ambush?"

"How should I know?! This is no time to panic!"

"Quit your blabberin' and fight back! We're packed together, but we can beat these guys to a pulp if we strike from the outside."

"All right, you radish fighters. Let's show 'em what we're made of!"

Jaeger's crimson armor clanged as he hefted a sword larger than himself onto his shoulder. Shining Saber and Cohral grinned ferociously and followed suit. Several players set their own oversized large swords on their shoulders and crouched into position.

"Why radishes?" Quolkeh asked without thinking.

"He's referring to a large sword for beginners that is white with a green hilt," Hidden Ogre replied, a halberd in each hand.

"Ah, got it." Nodding, Quolkeh took a whip in each hand and began slicing the wind in circles.

As each individual in the vanguard readied their technique, Cayna and the rest of the rearguard prepared attack magic beforehand. Sahana cast spells like DEX Up that would help the swordfighters strike true. As soon as everyone received this effect, the chimeras moved all at once.

"SHOW NO MERCYYYYY!!"

Everyone raced toward the black wave and unleashed a slew of sword techniques.

Flaming Bomb Lea Vork

Flame Snake Stampede Leala Barcia

A blazing ball of fire struck its target and scorched everything within a five-meter radius, while a flaming snake coiled around a different foe and burned it to cinders. Such magical attacks continued one after the other, but they only struck the monsters one row back so the vanguard wouldn't get caught up in it.

Cayna and Sahana's combined Mega Levork took things a step further. It blasted away not just monsters but the surrounding buildings and environment as well.

Weapon Skill: Sand Dragon Breakdown Storm

Jaeger, Shining Saber, and the other swordfighters dashed straight ahead. Their blades whirled like vigorous hammer throws and hit speeds invisible to the naked eye.

The wind began to swirl and rage around each and transformed the weapons into a single tornado. Several of the swordfighters' fierce twisters crowded together and tore through the approaching dark wave. The zigzag attack shredded anything in its path. Monsters were sliced sideways into several layers as the violent storm threw chunks of flesh into the sky. Enemies caught between two at the same time were shredded like paper. Monsters that once howled and trembled in delight as they swooped down on their quarry now shrieked in anguish.

Weapon Skill: Canyon Grind

Hidden Ogre held two large halberds in front of him and struck the earth in a circular sector. The cobblestones caught in a radial pattern caved in, and a stream of monsters lost their balance as they were swallowed up by the earth. Some panicked and tried to jump to freedom, but it was already too late.

Stone spears rose from below like billowing waves and pierced the captured monsters. Impaled by crude stone spears like a butcherbird's prey for later consumption, Hidden Ogre's foes were swiftly vanquished. Some did manage to escape but were either cut in half or burned to ashes by a wave of other players.

Weapon Skill: Rapid-Fire Spiral Slicer

Several players wielded a whip like Quolkeh, and their high-speed rotations produced wind buzz saws. Any monster that tried to forcibly squeeze through a gap in their technique was cut to ribbons. Each was carved into four or five unrecognizable slices and tossed into the air. This technique was more cost-effective than those that prioritized destructive power; you could strike multiple enemies at once, and it was easy to control. They coiled around the swordfighters' earlier tornadoes like drill bits, and the additional power aided the rush of players.

Magic Skill: Lea Lance Vision: Ready Set

Countless flame spears about two meters long appeared above Sahana's and Spirale's heads.

"Fire!"

"Go!"

The spears soared over the tornadoes and players to pierce the back row of monsters. Instead of burning, they instantly turned to ash and crumbled away without even time to scream.

Sahana had ample MP, so her shower of flame spears covered the entire blockade of monsters. Not a single foe who ran out of pure instinct avoided their dusty fate.

Eliminating the monsters took fifteen minutes from start to finish.

"Awww, it's over already? I was about to unleash my second attack, too..." Cayna looked ready for more action.

"If we left it to you, dear Cayna, none of us would get a turn." Spirale shouldered his wand with a grin.

"Kuu didn't get to attack," the fairy mumbled.

"Huh? Sissy, can that fairy fight, too?" Sahana's eyes widened in shock.

"She's so dangerous, even Opus runs for the hills."

"You're kidding…"

Cayna looked away with a defeated smile. Sahana didn't know what to believe.

"That aside, you should probably see to *them* first," said Spirale.

""What?""

The girls turned in the direction Spirale indicated with his wand and came upon a pleasant scene.

"Hrgh, hold…on… Blargh!"

"Ohhhh…"

"Ugh, I feel sick…"

There were only a few injuries, but the swordfighters suffered far differently from everyone else. Unsurprisingly, unlike back in the game where the players could fight as they pleased, the high speeds made most dizzy and pale with nausea. Wildly chopping up monsters was all fine and good, but the rain of meat chunks and blood splatters soon dyed them red and purple. Anyone who could use Purification cleaned them from head to toe.

"Ohhh?"

"Huh?"

While this was happening, a pillar of fire rose into the sky near the main entrance. Thanks to the Raid Link, each player was also enveloped in a red effect that granted Flame Resistance. The caster was Opus, who was still on his own.

Incidentally, several people heard some kind of howl and frowned.

"Wow, it sounds like a fight down there…," said Shining Saber.

"It truly pains me to say this, but I'm sure that rotten demon will be just fine."

"I knew it, Sahana," said Cayna. "You really do hate Opus..."

"Well, ya gotta figure he wouldn't be much help anyway. Let's leave him to it," Cohral suggested.

The group nodded in agreement. They had no desire to intentionally get involved in a tactician's battle.

Leaving a Limit Breaker to fight in a Limit Breaker's own way, they quickly pressed on to put this chaotic quest to rest.

"Onward! To a peaceful life!" Jaeger shouted.

""""YEAAAAAAAAAH————!!""""

With that, the players raced forward.

Character Data

Shining Saber

*Former sub-leader
of the Silver Moon
Horsemen Guild.
A level 472 silver
dragoid.*

Used to mainly swing his
sword on the front lines,
but now that he's a knight
captain, he's saddled
with a tedious amount of
paperwork. Things were
rough starting out: He first
appeared in this world in
the middle of a knights'
training ground and was
arrested on sight. After
landing some support, he
rose from soldier to knight
and then finally to knight
captain (his level improved
as well). Feels indebted to
Arbiter, a former knight
captain, as well as to his
own subordinates. The
knights firmly believe
Cayna is his fiancée, and
Shining Saber has failed
to dispel the rumors to
this day.

Cohral

Former member of the Silver Moon Horsemen Guild. A level 392 human.

Became an adventurer alongside the youths of the village that took him in, then joined a party called the Armor of Victory. Because of his high level, Cohral decided to become the party's defensive tank. The Armor of Victory helped him realize how suffocating his old life had been. He's aged a bit after ten years in this new world and is consequently more mentally mature than Shining Saber. Wants to get rid of his new title, Supreme Swordsman, as soon as possible.

Special Illustration Collection

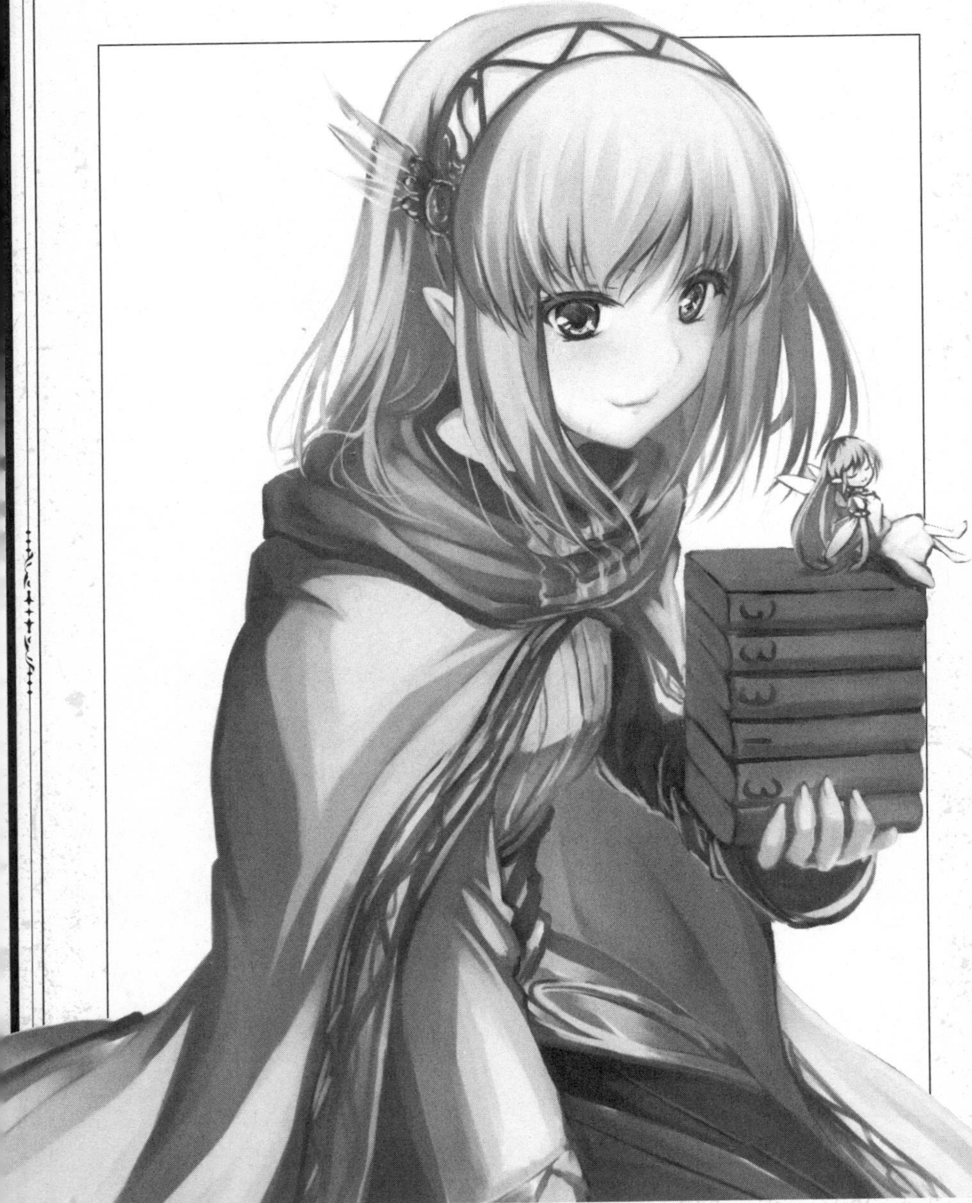

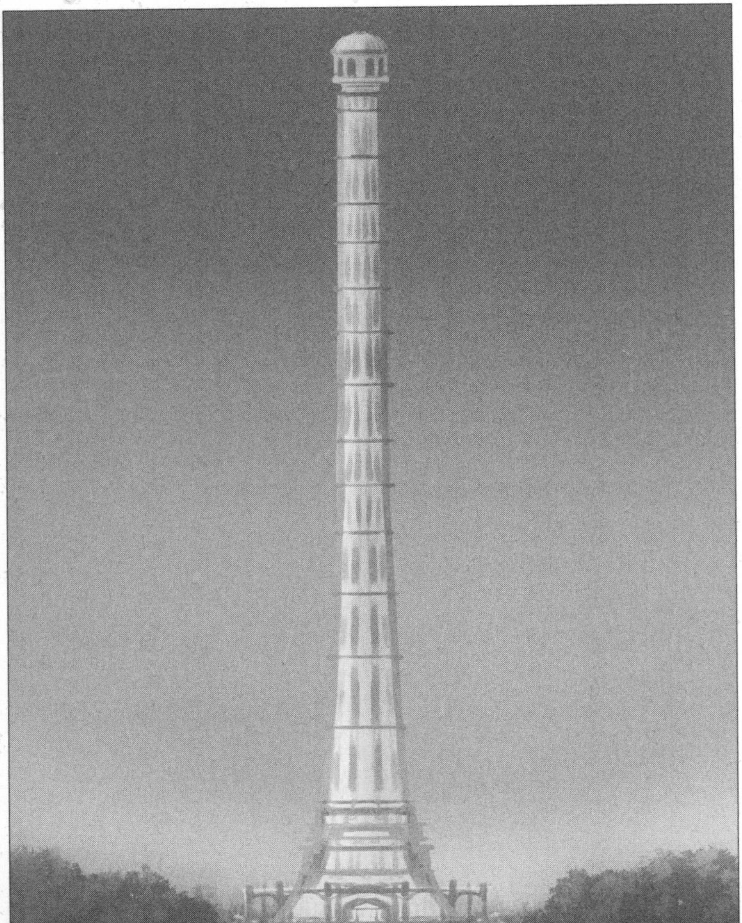

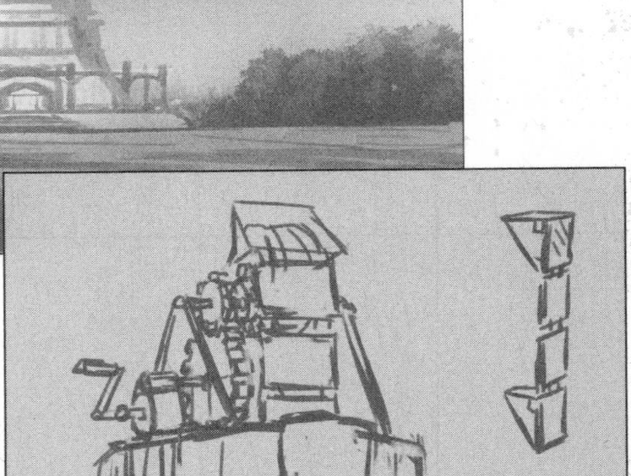

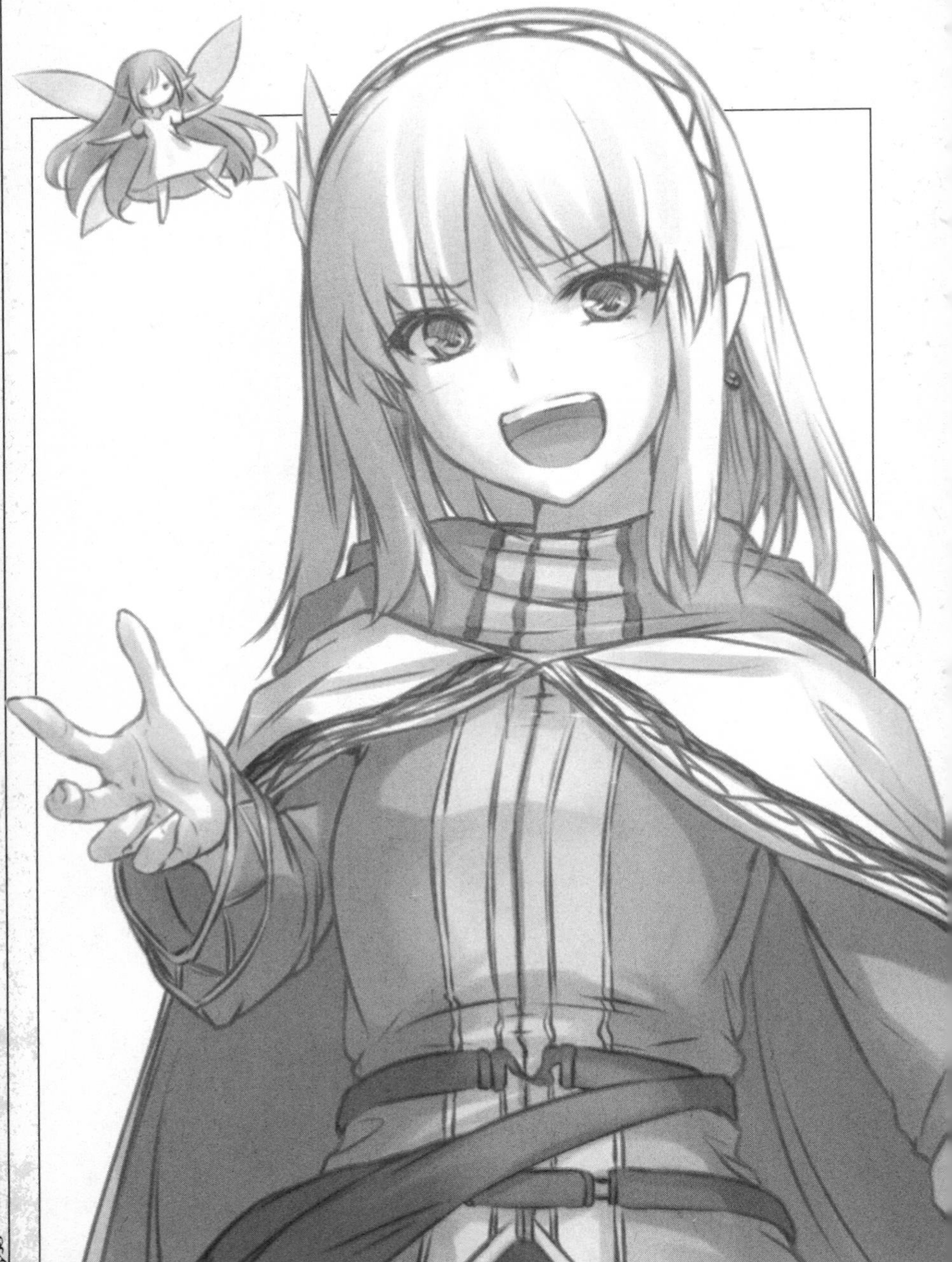

Afterword

Good morning, good afternoon, and good evening. I'm the author, Ceez. It looks like we've reached the tumultuous eighth volume. We've covered the first half of the event here, but I'm pretty sure it will conclude in the next volume. That's the plan.

Several episodes of the anime will already be out by the time this volume is released. I'm really nervous about everyone's impression! Ever since I began the series, I've always alternated between joy and fear over your opinions. I hope you'll find the anime uniquely charming.

I'd also like to take this opportunity express my deepest thanks to the director and all the staff involved. Looking back now, my editor first said the series would become an anime when the second volume just came out... I couldn't believe they contacted me.

Maho Films has a big mecha from a certain robot anime in their entrance, and I still think about it. Thank you so much to the fantastic voice actors who breathed life into these characters. We're still in difficult times, so I appreciate your willingness to record. I couldn't stop crying when I watched the final product before the official broadcast. I never would have dreamed this would happen to me when I first started the series ten years ago.

Furthermore, I caused so much trouble for everyone while writing this volume that it entirely negated my promise to do better in the last one. I'm soooo sorry! If it wasn't for the state of the world right now, I'd go on a pilgrimage of atonement.

My most heartfelt apologies to both my ever-patient editor and to the very busy illustrator Tenmaso for the long wait. I'm sorry for troubling the proofreader and book designer again as well. I'll do my best to stick to the next deadline...

Our unpredictable situation continues, but I hope everyone will continue to stick with me. I'm deeply grateful to all my readers!

Ceez

I'm the artist Tenmaso. The anime has started airing. Hopefully, somehow, I'll keep experiencing these kinds of nice moments in life.

Tenmaso

HAVE YOU BEEN TURNED ON TO LIGHT NOVELS YET?

86—EIGHTY-SIX, VOL. 1–11

In truth, there is no such thing as a bloodless war. Beyond the fortified walls protecting the eighty-five Republic Sectors lies the "nonexistent" Eighty-Sixth Sector. The young men and women of this forsaken land are branded the Eighty-Six and, stripped of their humanity, pilot "unmanned" weapons into battle...

Manga adaptation available now!

WOLF & PARCHMENT, VOL. 1–6

The young man Col dreams of one day joining the holy clergy and departs on a journey from the bathhouse, Spice and Wolf. Winfiel Kingdom's prince has invited him to help correct the sins of the Church. But as his travels begin, Col discovers in his luggage a young girl with a wolf's ears and tail named Myuri, who stowed away for the ride!

Manga adaptation available now!

SOLO LEVELING, VOL. 1–7

E-rank hunter Jinwoo Sung has no money, no talent, and no prospects to speak of—and apparently, no luck, either! When he enters a hidden double dungeon one fateful day, he's abandoned by his party and left to die at the hands of some of the most horrific monsters he's ever encountered.

Comic adaptation available now!